Mother's Daily Scream

Ann Pilling

Mother's
Daily Scream

VIKING

VIKING

Published by the Penguin Group
Penguin Books Ltd, 27 Wrights Lane, London W8 5TZ, England
Penguin Books USA Inc., 375 Hudson Street, New York, New York 10014, USA
Penguin Books Australia Ltd, Ringwood, Victoria, Australia
Penguin Books Canada Ltd, 10 Alcorn Avenue, Toronto, Ontario, Canada M4V 3B2
Penguin Books (NZ) Ltd, 182–190 Wairau Road, Auckland 10, New Zealand

Penguin Books Ltd, Registered Offices: Harmondsworth, Middlesex, England

First published 1995
1 3 5 7 9 10 8 6 4 2

Filmset in Monophoto Palatino
Typeset by Datix International Ltd, Bungay, Suffolk
Printed in England by Clays Ltd, St Ives plc

A CIP catalogue record for this book is available from the British Library

ISBN 0–670–85642–8

For my Godchildren
Jonathan and Rachel Atkinson

O n e

'You've got everything. I give you EVERY-THING! And what do I get in return? Abuse. Filth. You might as well defecate in the middle of the drawing-room. I repeat: I give you EVERY-THING!'

Up in his bedroom Jake shivered and Holly stretched out a comforting hand. Then a door slammed, two floors down, cutting off the terrible, screeching voice.

'What's she going on about?' whispered Holly. She was panicking. People didn't shout like that in her house.

Jake shrugged. 'Dunno. Don't ask me. S'pose she's just having one of her screams. She's always screaming.' He peered down vaguely at his feet. 'Perhaps it's this mud I brought in. Like my boots?'

He stuck out a foot for inspection. The boots, brand new, though their thick ridged soles were caked with something sticky and dark, were the colour of ginger cake, the laces chunky as ropes. The smell of the new leather was wonderful. Holly stroked them. She never ever had new things. But how had Jake got these? He'd told her that his mother was tight with money.

'Jacob? JACOB! Are you there? I'm going out. And don't ask me for any supper, because I'm not cooking for somebody so uncooperative.'

'Oh, drop dead,' he said under his breath.

Holly giggled. 'Muv has little screams sometimes,' she said, 'when she, you know, gets fed up of housework and things, but not, well, it's not like . . .' Having started the sentence she felt suddenly embarrassed and her voice fizzled into nothing.

'Not like a police-car siren? Huh. She used to be in a big choir. Pity she doesn't go back to it. She could scream her head off there. Listen, can we go to your place? She'll only come and get me if I stay here.'

'What do you mean, "get you"?' Holly asked curiously.

Laura, Jake's mother, was quite large. She had dark red hair, very thick, plaited and rolled up in a fat bun on top of her head. Her eyes, like Muv's, were brown, but there all resemblance ended. Mrs Berry would never scream about mud on the carpet, she'd merely sweep it up and say nothing. Anyhow, they didn't have carpet in the hall at the vicarage, just nasty brown lino. Mrs Tolland, Jake's mother, had hard, glittery little eyes. Holly always felt she was about to pounce on you. No wonder Jake talked about running away.

He said, 'Half the time I don't know what she's on about anyway. "You might as well *what* in the middle of the drawing-room?" Why does she have to go on as if she's swallowed the dictionary?'

Holly blushed. She knew what the word meant. 'We can look it up. There's a dictionary in my bedroom.'

Her room at the vicarage was used as a dumping ground for Farve's extra books. Once, a student lodger had painted the edges of the shelves red, and at night, sometimes, she fancied devilish red creatures with claws were crouching there, ready to pounce, like Jake's mum. She'd given up asking if the room could be redecorated. Muv and Farve had no money for fripperies like that.

There they sat, Holly and Jake. Jake Tolland and Holly Berry. Holly's real name was Hannah, but she didn't mind Holly. It had started off as a family joke, and stuck. She'd only ever minded it last year, when she'd first gone to the Comprehensive. Someone had found out about Farve being a vicar and had called her Holy Holly. She'd cornered that person, Sharon Bradley, in the lavatories. She'd seen red, managed to sit on her and given her a good thump. Nobody used the name again. You didn't quarrel with Holly Berry, people said afterwards. Actually, nobody liked Sharon much, and for a few days Holly became a bit of a hero.

She was tallish, but quite thickset. It was no joke if she sat on you. She had curly black hair framing a very pretty face, but she definitely looked stubborn. That's because she was. Her nose was little and neat, something that might have belonged to a pixie. But her chin made up for it. Very firm, Holly's chin was, with a cleft in it. It was a chin that meant business.

Jake had very bad spots. He was little and skinny, but he had a big head and a long straight nose. His ears stuck out. If Holly was a pixie then Jake was a gnome. They were best friends, always had been since that day at the Comprehensive when Holly had sat on Sharon Bradley, and Jake had stuck up for her with the teachers.

At school nobody could quite understand the Holly-Jake friendship. Were they boy-friend and girl-friend, everyone wanted to know, and did they kiss each other? Other people did, *and* more. Holly had started to explain. She'd said it wasn't like that, not with her and Jake. They were just friends. Jake was the same as her brother James, and it wasn't anything to do with kissing.

But she'd not liked the sneery looks or the sly giggling, and she'd absolutely hated Jake's embar-

4

rassed pink face, his mute, pleading stare when people started whispering about sex. They even went on about her being taller than him, as if that mattered.

Finally she'd lost her temper with them and their unpleasant, prying questions. 'Listen,' she'd announced one day in rather a dangerous voice, 'we're *friends*, just *friends*. Geddit? There's nothing interesting going on at all. Sorry to disappoint you.'

And that, she decided, was all she ever intended to say. What she and Jake did together, which was only talking, was nothing whatever to do with anybody else. Anyhow, if that was the way their minds were working, they'd never understand the real thing, that she and Jake seemed to need each other. Jake was an only child. Her brother James was away at school and came home as little as possible. They were both lonely.

Jake said, 'I'm hungry. Anything in at your house? My mother's doing Weight Watchers again. The fridge is empty.'

'*Absolutely* empty?' Holly felt slightly nervous. Jake had started hanging round the vicarage at mealtimes and Farve didn't approve. In fact, he didn't like Jake at all. This puzzled her. He was so good with all the weirdos that dropped into the vicarage, but he couldn't seem to tolerate Jake.

'Well, yes,' Jake told her, 'apart from skimmed milk and a bag of carrot sticks. Laura says I've got to get my own food this week.'

'That's a bit mean.'

Jake's mouth turned down at the corners. 'She says as long as I smoke she won't feed me.'

'That makes sense. Smoking's bad for you.'

'Listen,' he said angrily, 'I need to smoke. It calms me down.'

Holly got up. This was always how their worst arguments began. 'Come on, we can go to my house. But you'd better take those boots off. You don't want her yelling at you again when she gets back.'

They crept down the stairs with their shoes in their hands, down a soft grey carpet so deep and lush you felt it might swallow you up, like a swamp. The staircase was quaintly narrow with pretty white banisters, the walls a soft pink, hung with pictures in thin gold frames. As you turned corners there were plants flowing out of copper tubs, or hanging artistically from bamboo poles screwed to the ceiling. It was all lovely, lovely. Every time Holly saw 17, Addison Mews, the house took her breath away. THE HOUSE. That was how Mrs Tolland talked about it, in capital letters. It seemed to be the most important thing in her life, more important than Jake, or the boy-friends who appeared from time to time. (Jake's dad? Who was he? He'd walked out long ago and Jake never saw him. He lived with a girl-friend in Spain.)

The walls were quite close together and to get downstairs without touching them and therefore risking SMUDGES and DIRTY MARKS you had to make yourself very thin, in fact you had to THINK THIN. (Holly knew all about thinking thin. Muv had done Weight Watchers too.) Obligingly she scrunched her shoulders together, but Jake didn't care. He flicked at the banisters as he came down, playing a little tune and, Holly thought, making at least two smudges. When he got into the hall he lit a cigarette.

'Don't, Jake,' she said, 'don't make her mad.'

'Well, *I'm* mad. Can't you see that?' As they came down the front steps into the street he seemed close to tears.

'Now come *on*.' Holly tucked her arm in his and marched him down the street. He was little and she was big, but what did it matter? People mattered, and he was upset. 'People matter more than things.' That's what Muv and Farve were always telling her. She'd still like a lovely room though, a big white room like Jake's. But he'd made it so awful with his overflowing ashtrays and his sweaty bedding, all the CDs and videos thrown around, and sticky patches on the polished floor. His mum really shouldn't have stuck that notice on the door though, the notice that said DO NOT FEED THE RATS. No wonder they had these screaming matches.

'I've got to go to the supermarket,' she told him as they crossed the bridge over the canal. 'Hang on. I've got a list.'

'Let's have a look.' Jake had cheered up instantly. He was keen on shops.

'It's boring. Bacon, eggs — that's for tea — toilet paper, black shoe polish . . . that's all . . . oh no, bread.'

'Shoe polish on toast,' Jake said thoughtfully. 'What about beans? I like baked beans with eggs and bacon.'

'Not on the list.'

'They're cheap, beans.'

'But they're not on the list. Farve gets annoyed if I get things that aren't on the list. He has to work out our money.'

Jake pulled a sour face and followed her into the supermarket. He'd never much liked Holly's dad. He was all rules and regulations, like in school. While she got the shopping he sauntered up and down the aisles pulling things off shelves and putting them back again. Then he disappeared somewhere. At the checkout he turned up again, with a small chocolate bar and a fifty pence piece to pay for it.

'Want a bit?' he said as they walked along the canal. The towpath was smelly and lonely, but it was the quickest way to Museum Road and St Bartholomew's vicarage.

'No thanks.'

'Thought you liked chocolate?'

'I do. I'm a chocoholic. But Muv doesn't buy it any more, so I'm trying to get to like diet things.'

'Go on. Have some.' Secretly, Jake's admiration of Holly in this determined mood was unbounded. He wasn't strong-willed like her.

'NO!' she said in a loud voice.

Suddenly he stopped. She had noticed big bulges in his side pockets and now he pulled out two green tins. 'There you are. Baked beans. A fry-up's not a fry-up without baked beans.'

Holly stared. 'But you . . . Jake, you didn't buy these in Bailey's.'

'No.'

'So how did you . . .?'

'Nicked them, didn't I?'

Holly's mouth dropped open. 'You mean you *stole* them?'

Jake flushed. 'Well, they didn't walk off the shelf and climb into my pockets on their own, did they? It was easy. They're pathetic in Bailey's. They deserve to get things nicked in that shop.'

Holly took the two tins and dropped them into

her carrier-bag. Then she set off again along the towpath, back towards the supermarket. Jake came after her and grabbed the bag. 'What are you doing?'

'Taking them back. We can't keep them.'

'You can't take them back, not now. I *mean* . . .'

'All right. You take them back. You stole them.'

'It's not stealing.'

'What is it then?'

Jake lit a cigarette. 'Well, it's just . . . oh, for goodness' *sake*, Holly, who cares about a load of baked beans?' and he threw them into the flat, oily waters of the Bridgewater Canal.

Holly stared into the murk of the rainy summer afternoon as they plopped out of sight. 'I see,' she said slowly and, picking up the shopping, she set off for the vicarage. Jake stayed at the water's edge sucking on his cigarette.

'Can I still come round?' he called after her. His voice, floating along the water, sounded thin and desperate.

'Suit yourself,' she said coldly, and walked solidly on.

T w o

It was Tuesday. The pig was on the table. This pig was made of black pottery and it had a slit in its back where everyone had to put their spare pennies, to give to the drop-ins. It was enormous and very smug-looking. It was called Napoleon.

Pig-on-the-Table meant that if Holly looked in Muv's Safe Place she would find a message. Farve worried about burglars, not that there was anything much to burgle at the vicarage, so the Safe Place changed from week to week. Sometimes it was behind some tins of soup in the pantry. Sometimes it was under the lino by the front door. This time it was easy. The Safe Place was third drawer down in the kitchen dresser.

Muv's note was complicated and obviously written in a rush. Something about Fat Nan having to go to hospital, they'd all gone with her, Muv, Farve *and* N.O.P. No problems, said the note, nothing to worry about, just a regular appointment.

But Farve had taken them in his car because Fat Nan couldn't climb on to buses any more.

Jake seemed relieved to find the house empty. He wandered about fiddling with things while Holly put away the shopping. Since the beans had gone into the canal they hadn't spoken. He'd just followed her home into the vicarage.

'Funny smell,' he said, wrinkling up his nose. 'What is it?'

'I don't know. And it's rude to make personal remarks.'

'Sorry,' Jake said humbly. He sat at the table and tried to make himself as small and as inoffensive as possible. He didn't want to be sent away. He liked it at Holly's. He felt safe there. He liked the feel of a mum and a dad, of people who were always there for you, even though the dad was a bit fierce and unfriendly.

Holly did know what the smell was. It was Old Lady. Before, it had just been Old House and general dirt. The place was far too big for Muv to keep clean, and although they now had Doris to come and help it didn't seem to make any difference.

What was different was their grandmother, Fat Nan. She was Farve's mother and a few months ago she'd come to live with them, in two rooms off the hall, which they used to rent out to students.

12

It wasn't that Holly didn't like her grandmother. Really, she hardly knew her. She'd lived with Thin Gramps up in Scotland and they hadn't met very often. But now Thin Gramps had died and Fat Nan was ill. She was old too, and when you got old, Muv said, you couldn't always get to the loo in time. That was the smell. Muv used loads of disinfectant and air freshener, but somehow . . . she wasn't telling Jake though. It wasn't fair on Fat Nan.

The Fat Nan smell was mixed with a smell of baby. N.O.P. liked throwing her food around when she sat in her high chair, and the bits that stuck to the ceiling just stayed there. Then there were the nappies, lurking in corners in various buckets. One way and another St Bartholomew's vicarage was a smelly place.

N.O.P. was Holly's baby sister. Her proper name was Ruth. Only Holly and her brother James called her N.O.P. and that was because James had found out that she wasn't meant to be born. This is how he'd found out. Muv and Farve once had some friends to stay, friends that had been students with them at college. James had been going up to bed and the front-room door was open. They were all laughing and Farve had opened a bottle of wine. Then Ruth had started grizzling, up in her cot, and he'd heard Muv explain that they *did* love Ruthie, but that really she wasn't meant to have happened. She'd said to Farve, 'It was a night of passion, wasn't it, sweetheart?' So that was how Ruth came to be called N.O.P. (Night of Passion) between Holly and James. But it was an absolute secret.

Holly liked James, but she was jealous of him. She went to the Comprehensive at Arnold's Green and he went to boarding-school, to a place called St Wilfred's. Holly, whose favourite books were the Malory Towers ones, had always longed to go to a school like that. It had green fields all round it and, at the end of the fields, the sea. There was a swimming-pool and a huge gymnasium and, oh, *everything*. James loved it. All his school-friends seemed to live in mansions with fields and swimming-pools too. Holly suspected that he had got rather a taste for big houses with swimming-pools, for big cars and horses. She noticed that he never brought his friends home here, to the vicarage, and that whenever he could he accepted invitations to go away for the holidays. Muv and Farve never said anything about it. They were very loyal, both of them. They seemed glad he had such wonderful friends. But she was certain that they *did* mind because, when he wrote to ask about these invitations, Muv always looked a bit sad, and Farve usually shut himself in his study. Perhaps, then, wonderful schools like St Wilfred's turned out snobs, sometimes. Perhaps it wasn't a good idea for Holly to go to one, though she'd always longed to.

Anyhow, there was no money for her. James only went to St Wilfred's because Farve was a vicar and some charity thing paid. Still, one good thing that had come out of it was her getting to know Jake. He'd started off at St Wilfred's too and at first he wasn't at the Comprehensive with all the other new ones. Then St Wilfred's said he couldn't stay there any more. He was sent home to Laura and told not to come back. This didn't suit Mrs Tolland at all. The House wasn't intended for human habitation, just to look at. Anyway, he'd ended up at Holly's school, though quite often he just didn't go. His mother was away a lot and didn't seem to know what he did with his time. Just why he'd left St Wilfred's was a mystery. 'Nobody says why,' Muv told her, wearing her 'don't-ask-me' face. She obviously knew, but she wasn't going to tell lies. Now Holly wondered if it was something to do with stealing.

'Can we have the bacon and eggs then?' Jake said. He was ravenous. His insides were meeting in the middle. All he'd had for dinner was low-fat cheese sandwiches and a diet yoghurt.

Holly looked shocked. 'Well, no,' she said, 'not till Muv and Farve get back.'

'But why not? Listen, I'll do it. Where's the

frying-pan?' and he started rooting about in a cupboard.

Holly stopped him. 'You *mustn't*.'

'Can't you cook then?'

She hesitated. 'Course I can. But it's frying. That can be dangerous. My father says ... anyhow, it's not tea-time.' The idea of frying eggs and bacon for Jake Tolland in a house where meals appeared at set times was appalling. What would Farve say? And especially for *Jake*. 'We can have a peanut-butter sandwich,' she said. 'That's allowed.'

Ungraciously, Jake grunted. 'OK. Let's have that then.'

He watched her spreading slices of bread with low-fat marge. So both their mothers were dieting. His was doing it to impress Daniel, the new boy-friend. He made films for TV and drove a BMW. Jake longed for chip sandwiches, hamburgers, sausage and mash. But all that belonged to the good old days, when Dad had lived with them and he and Laura had seemed to love each other, when the House was just a semi in an ordinary road and Dad hadn't made all that money. When there was no screaming.

Holly's vicarage was scruffy and it had a funny smell, but at least it was peaceful. They climbed the stairs. 'Why do you —'

'Shh . . .' Holly hissed, as they crept past a firmly shut door. 'There's someone asleep in there.'

'Who?'

'I don't know. One of the drop-ins. A new one.'

'D'you mind all these weird people in your house?' They had reached Holly's attic room, a small pointy affair with a pointy ceiling and even pointier windows. It was dark, papered with large, faded roses, and the cream paint was peeling. All the flat bits of wall were lined with books. Only a few belonged to Holly. The rest were her father's. It was very, very tidy compared with Jake's room, but it was very dingy too. He'd hate having a bedroom like this.

'Course I mind.' Holly took an aggressive bite out of her sandwich. 'I mean, wouldn't you? I never know who's here. Yesterday I was in the loo — the lock's broken — and this tramp person walked in. Farve had brought him home from the Centre.'

'What did you do?'

'Nothing. I just sat there. He was quite nice actually. He just went away. Ooh, he did stink though.'

It seemed to Jake that everything had a stink in this house. And it seemed too that nobody could win, in the end. Either you were stuck with Laura, madly doing up her precious House and having a

17

nervous breakdown if you got mud on the carpet, or you were stuck with people like Holly's Muv and Farve. They obviously didn't care about houses at all, and that was good, in a way, but they were so busy looking after drop-in types and tramps, that Holly got no attention. Now her grandmother had come to stay as well. He'd hate that. He wasn't too keen on babies either. Holly had a lot to put up with.

He said slowly, 'You might as well . . . *what* in the middle of the drawing-room?' He could still hear his mother's awful, high-pitched scream. It sent shivers down his back.

Holly stood on a chair and managed to lift an enormous dictionary down from one of the red-devil shelves. She looked through it, flapping pages, then she stopped. 'There you are. What she's actually saying is —'

Jake followed her finger. 'Oh, I see. It means —'

'It means what Ruthie calls the Big Poo.'

Jake recoiled and slammed the book shut. Then he started pacing round the attic. 'How disgusting. How disgusting of my mother. She was saying I was so foul I might as well . . . go to the toilet in the middle of the carpet.'

'Yep.'

'That really is disgusting. I mean, don't *you* think parents are disgusting?'

Holly looked thoughtful and put her head on one side. 'I suppose . . . well, sometimes mine get on my nerves.'

But Jake wasn't really listening. He was thinking about his own mother. 'I mean, the way she nags me, she just goes on and on and ON. About things that don't matter, little things, like chucking my duvet on the floor when I get hot, or leaving a few mugs on the carpet. She doesn't understand that a creative person like me *needs* a certain degree of mess. And it's not doing her any harm. All that screaming. There's never a day passes without her screaming at me.'

'The Daily Scream,' Holly said quietly. 'All parents have to have their daily scream. Nan gets the *Daily Mail*. Farve pretends he doesn't like it but he always grabs it first. He reads it before he reads his *Times*.'

'"You're not the centre of the universe",' said Jake in a silly, high-pitched voice.

Holly stared at him. His sharp nose and high, thin cheeks made his whole face grow to a point. His eyes had a glassy faraway look. 'That's one of the things she says.'

'"Money doesn't grow on trees",' he added, the silly voice getting sillier. 'That's another.'

'My father says that too.'

'Does he? Laura says it every single day. Mind

19

you, you'd think it did – grow on trees, I mean – she's always buying antiques, for the house.'

'But she did buy you those gorgeous boots.'

Jake swallowed and the lump in his throat clicked in and out. Slowly he turned pink and there was a silence. Holly started wondering about the boots. He'd stolen the baked beans from Bailey's. What other things might he have taken from shops? But how did he actually do it? Had he walked out with the boots on his feet? And what had he done with his old shoes?

'"You don't know you're born". That's another thing my mother says. And I mean, we didn't *ask* to be born, did we? It's a ridiculous thing to say.'

'I agree,' Holly said stoutly. 'I absolutely agree.' Muv and Farve had never said quite such a pointless thing to her, but she didn't want to let Jake down, so she said nothing.

Jake rather fancied himself as a writer. He wrote poems sometimes. They were weird. No full stops or capital letters and the words often upside down. He could do drawings too, and he made up cartoons. It obviously all went with the mess in his room. It must be to do with his artistic temperament.

He said, 'Got any paper?'

Holly went to her old desk and produced a box. The paper was in little pink sheets, decorated with

20

hedgehogs. Fat Nan had given it to her. Jake inspected it and pulled a face. This kind of thing didn't seem quite right for the birth of a new national newspaper, but it was all she'd got so it would have to do. He had just decided to found a paper about awful parents. It would be called the *Daily Scream*.

Holly thought it was a brilliant idea. She settled down with some pink hedgehog paper too and got them both pencils.

'We need a really good headline,' she said. 'They always have those. You know, "Teenager eats baby in pie orgy."'

'Ugh.' Then Jake started scribbling. 'How about this? "Boy defecates in mother's drawing-room."'

'Oh, *Jake*...'

'All right then. No big words ... er ... "Teenager goes to toilet on new carpet"?'

Holly giggled. 'Listen, we can do the main headline later, but what's going to go in this paper?'

Jake chewed his pencil. '"Sayings of the Week" definitely. And we should leave it lying around, so they *know* how they get on our nerves.'

'Advice,' said Holly. 'We ought to give people advice. "How to handle your parents", that kind of thing.'

'I don't know how to handle mine,' Jake said bleakly.

'Listen. Shut up for a minute and don't be so pathetic. Write your ideas down. I'll write mine. They'll be back from the hospital in a minute and we'll have to put all this away.'

'But why?'

'Because Farve snoops.'

'So does Laura.'

Holly started writing. '" Are your parents snoopers?" That's another article,' she said. Then she giggled again. 'We could have a serial, a chapter each week. "Night of Passion" — how does that sound?'

'Great. But what are you laughing at?'

'Oh, just something.'

There was quiet, while they wrote things. And so, in Holly's pointy attic with its faded, peeling roses, the *Daily Scream* was born. So were other things, very big things. But at the time neither Jake nor Holly knew anything about them. If they had known they might have been scared.

Three

Tuesday night was 'Diary Time' at the vicarage. Diary Time had been invented by Farve. It was when everyone sat round and explained what they were going to do for the rest of the week. Sunday was church all day, then Monday was Farve's day off, except that he never seemed to take a day off any more. So Tuesday was the official start of the week.

Jake had gone home, after the eggs and bacon. Farve hadn't fussed about him staying for tea but he'd not been very friendly. And afterwards he'd told Holly that he didn't much like Jake coming round. The excuse was Fat Nan. 'Nanna adds to the pressures on your mother,' he said. Holly knew this wasn't true. Muv fed anyone who came to the vicarage, including the drop-ins and the tramps. Farve simply didn't like Jake.

He obviously thought he was a 'bad influence' on Holly, and might lead her into bad ways. His kid sister, Auntie Linda, had come under bad influences when she was young. She'd run away from home with a boy from her school, had a baby, become a kind of traveller, and never came home again to her parents. Auntie Linda was the black sheep of Farve's family, though when she'd met her, Holly had liked her a lot. She was really good fun, always cracking jokes. And she'd taken Holly to the fair.

Jake though . . . What on earth would Farve say if he found out about the baked beans? And the boots? Something told Holly that those wonderful boots *had* been stolen.

'So what are you doing with yourself, chicken?' Muv asked her. Sometimes Holly was 'chicken' and sometimes 'duckie'. Other times she was just 'pet'. Muv was like a hen, little and round with soft, fluffy hair. Holly liked to snuggle up against her, but now she was taller than her mother, so it felt funny. Farve didn't hug her very often, just gave her a remote goodnight kiss before she went to bed, with, 'Don't forget to say your prayers, Holly,' added to it. Holly never said her prayers. She didn't know how to any more. So many sad things happened; she was always seeing them on the TV news. She thought it was awful how Thin Gramps had died and Fat Nan had had the stroke. She didn't like to think of Fat Nan too much, all big and helpless and quiet. Farve was sad about it too. Fat Nan was his mother, after all.

Everyone had a diary except N.O.P., who was sitting in her high chair flinging food about while they talked. Farve's week consisted of endless meetings and services. Muv had about a million people to visit and when she wasn't visiting she was helping clean the church and doing the bookstall and making meals for people. Holly hadn't got anything much to do, apart from 'jobs' dished out by Farve. There were always a lot of those. She didn't think it was fair, but she didn't like to say anything. Farve sulked if she did and said she was 'ungrateful', and it only meant that Muv had to do everything. Anyhow, she had plenty of time to do things. It was the start of the summer holidays, but her only trip away was a weekend camping with the Guides.

Farve had some news about James. His school had finished, but he'd gone straight off to an adventure centre in Wales. They were going to climb mountains and sleep rough. It sounded much better than going away with the 11th Darnley-in-Makerfield Guide Company. Then he'd been invited to go on holiday with his best friend, David. They had a big house in Scotland, a house on a river. The plan was to go on fishing trips with David's dad.

'I'd like him to go,' Farve said, though he looked very fed up when he said it, and so did Muv. 'It's a great opportunity. It's wonderful country up there.'

'But what about us?' Holly said in a small voice. 'Aren't we having a holiday?' Under the kitchen table Muv squeezed her hand.

'Well, it's tricky.' Farve's voice had gone reedy and thin. It was his nervous voice, the voice he used when he had a hard message to deliver. 'I've got the patronal festival, as usual, but this time it's going to be big. It's four hundred years since they built the first church here. I think the bishop might come. They're even talking of using the old plate. So till *that's* over I can't get my mind round summer holidays, I'm afraid.'

Muv gave Holly's hand another squeeze. 'We'll go somewhere, pet. Promise. Only Daddy's right, the festival is important this year. You understand, don't you?'

'Course.'

'And it's all right if James goes to David's?'

'Course.'

'Good girl. Listen, tell you what, we'll go out for days.'

'OK.'

Holly wanted to cry. 'Going out for days' was no good. They'd done that when N.O.P. was born. Muv couldn't drive and Farve was always busy. It meant taking sandwiches, nearly always put together by Holly, and going somewhere on a bus, some 'beauty spot', where they joined hundreds of other people and went on tame little walks, trudging through the litter. Before N.O.P. had arrived people had loaned them holiday cottages, awful places most of them. Holly was convinced that somewhere in the world there was a Holiday Cottage Shop. It sold the following things: very thin curtains that let the light in and woke you up far too early; damp beds; mugs with 'A Present from Scarborough' stamped on them, usually chipped; dim lightbulbs; atrocious weather. She couldn't think of one family holiday that she'd enjoyed. This year there clearly wasn't going to *be* a family holiday. Well, she thought rebelliously, that was all right by her.

Anyhow, Farve made excuses every year. He always blamed the patronal festival, the feast of their saint, St Bartholomew. On 'his' day there were a lot of services followed by an elaborate tea-party. But she didn't understand all this about the bishop and the fuss about an old plate.

'We have a very valuable paten,' Farve said, 'the plate we use for communion. It's gold. It's in the bank. Most of the stuff like that was melted down in the days of Oliver Cromwell, but someone buried this one. We think we might use it, just this once.'

27

'How exciting,' said Muv. She always encouraged Farve. He got so depressed about his church, especially when people didn't come to services, and nobody came much.

Holly said nothing. She disapproved. She thought religion ought to be much simpler. Jesus's friends were fishermen, they wouldn't have had gold plates. They were beggars, really. But at least Farve wouldn't force her to go to this feast. He wasn't that bad. She only had to go to church at Easter. What she really longed for, though, was to have a real *Christmas*. But Farve didn't believe in it. They'd never been allowed to have Father Christmas and stockings because he thought things like that got children muddled about Jesus Christ. So Christmas Day was pretty ordinary at St Bartholomew's vicarage, except that Farve was out doing services all day.

It was about Christmas that he'd had his one quarrel with Muv. She'd always gone along with his idea. But when N.O.P. arrived she said she'd rather like Christmas for once, with a tree and everything. Farve had sulked and said she didn't 'support' him and Muv had cried and said, 'I do. I *do.*'

Holly didn't listen while Muv and Farve were going through their diaries. She just switched off. She'd decided once and for all that she wasn't going to get married, not if it meant being like Muv. It wasn't that Farve didn't love her, and they never quarrelled, apart from the once, about Christmas. But Farve treated Muv like a doormat. He said how things were going to be and that was that. Now she had Nan to look after as well as N.O.P. If you added all the church things it meant she didn't have time to be a person in her own right. Everyone ought to have time for that, Holly had decided.

That night she broke two rules. First, she made a phone call to Jake, without asking, on Muv and Farve's bedroom extension. And, while Muv was seeing to Fat Nan and Dad was talking to one of the drop-ins, she went out. Holly wasn't supposed to go out at night without asking permission and she absolutely wasn't supposed to walk along the canal towpath. But that was the quickest way to Jake's.

Diary Time and the big let-down about the summer had made her think more about Jake. OK, his mother nagged and screamed, but at least she gave him space to be a person, even if it was accidental, even if it was because she was more interested in being with her latest boyfriend. Life at the vicarage was a bit *safe*, with Muv and Farve and three meals a day. Sometimes, too, the way her parents went on, looking after the drop-outs, must surely strike the outside world as a bit 'goody-

goody'. Jake, she felt, lived more in the real world. He wasn't always happy but, somehow, the freedom he had, to do what he liked, attracted her. And it was so lovely at his house. She wanted to see all the beautiful things.

She also wanted to talk to him about the stealing. It appalled her, but it fascinated her too. So she left two pillows mounded up in her bed, just in case Muv peeped in, and slid away. The mud along the towpath was slippy and once she slid very near the edge. That went deep, somehow. It was as if Jake was pulling her away from the good things, as if she was sliding towards badness and revolution.

Well, Muv had always said, 'Our Holly's a bit of a rebel.' Perhaps it was coming true. Perhaps she'd end up like bad Auntie Linda, who'd run away from home and had never come back. That would make them think.

Four

As she turned the corner and came into Addison Mews a shouting match was in progress. Laura, Jake's mum, was nowhere to be seen but Jake was standing on the pavement arguing with Mr Horne, who lived next door. The old man appeared to be weeping.

'I just can't stand another minute of it,' he was whimpering. 'I'd call the police again, but they say it's none of their business. I'm having a nervous breakdown. Where's your mother?'

Music was coming from the House, pop music, pop music so loud Holly felt she could almost see the pretty trellised walls pulsating in and out. She marched up to Jake. 'Switch it off,' she demanded loudly. 'Can't you see he's upset?'

Jake thrust his lower lip out. 'Why should I? He's exaggerating, as usual. He's trying to get me into trouble with Laura again. He enjoys getting me into trouble.'

'It's all right, Mr Horne, I'll fix it.' Holly walked up to the front door, went into the drawing-room and pulled out every plug she could see. Silence. Then, through the wall, a door slammed shut. Mr Horne had obviously gone home.

Jake came in. 'Take your boots off. TAKE YOUR BOOTS OFF!' Holly yelled at him. It was raining. They could do without a repeat of Mud on the Carpet.

He pulled off the marvellous boots and chucked them into a corner, knocking a fern over. Then he stomped off to the kitchen muttering, 'I'm hungry. Why is there never anything to *eat* in this place?'

Holly followed him, looking with interest round the dreamy space-age kitchen while Jake foraged. On the fridge was a graph. 'Laura's Progress : from Fattypuff to Thinifer.' The line was depressingly straight, no dips or swoops.

'Doesn't look as if your mum's making much progress.'

'No. Daniel — that's the boy-friend — keeps taking her to try out new restaurants.'

The fridge was very interesting. A newspaper cutting from the *Independent* said 'Tests Prove That Loud Music Can Permanently Damage Hearing' (Laura). Underneath was written 'Who Cares?' (Jake). Another bedroom door notice had appeared.

THE RATS HAVE MOVED IN. BEWARE (Laura). And underneath that, 'SO WHAT?' (Jake).

In the freezer was a Chinese TV-dinner for two. Jake took it out and read the instructions. 'I'm going to microwave this. Do you want some?'

'Well, OK . . . How many calories though?'

'Listen. If you're going to start that you can go home. I have enough of that with my mother.'

'Sorry,' Holly said meekly. She didn't want to go home. She was in rebellion. And she wanted to sit in Laura Tolland's beautiful drawing-room.

It was less beautiful than usual. Jake had thrown his boots off, and his socks, and his leather jacket, and she counted four coffee mugs on various perches. The fern had fallen over, spilling soft black earth on to the carpet and there was a strong smell of cigarettes. 'Is your mother coming home to-night?' she said.

'Dunno. Shouldn't think so. Think she's having — what did you call it — a Night of Passion. Thought any more about the *Daily Scream*?'

'A bit. I wondered if Night of Passion, I mean the serial, could be done from our baby's point of view, something like, "My name is Ruth Berry, I am eighteen months old. I'm only on this earth because of a Night of Passion. My favourite food is rusks. My favourite occupation is throwing food at the ceiling. Muv claps when I do a nice poo in my potty . . ." What do you think?'

Jake grinned. 'Sounds OK. Might win the Newspaper of the Year Award.'

'What about you then?'

'Well, papers have handy tips don't they? I thought we might use Doris, y'know, "Doris's Handy Hints".' He pulled a face. 'She's coming tomorrow. And I've spent the money Laura left for her. You couldn't lend me ten pounds could you?'

Holly's mouth dropped open. She had never, ever *seen* ten pounds, not all at once anyhow. 'What have you spent all that on? Cigarettes?'

Jake looked vague and shuffled about. 'Take a look at this then.' He held out a small smooth black object, a bit like a carpet cutter's knife.

'What is it?'

'It's a desk organizer. They're the latest thing. It has scissors, like this, and a Biro, and a knife, like this, and a screwdriver. This is where you use the thing for getting stones out of horses' hoofs, and this is where you put the bits when you sharpen pencils and this is where –'

'Did you spend the ten pounds on it?' Holly was not impressed. She would never, in her wildest imaginings, want a desk organizer.

'Suppose I did.'

Holly looked at him and knew he was lying. 'I

think you stole it. I think it came from that new paper shop on the Parade. I saw them there. They were next to the sweets.'

Jake stared out of the window. Holly was thinking, '*Why* does he steal things? He doesn't really need them. He threw those baked beans away. And this desk organizer's just a fad. He'll probably never use it. Does he get a kind of kick out of it? Or does he want someone to catch him doing it? Is it because his mother takes no notice of him? She'd have to, if the police came knocking on the door.'

She decided to change the subject.

'You know Doris has started to come to us as well, don't you? Nan pays. It's funny. Muv tries to clean up before she arrives. Cleaning up for the cleaning lady. It's ridiculous.'

'Laura doesn't think she's any good,' said Jake. 'She doesn't do the corners properly. She calls her the dirtying lady. She won't last. My mother gets through two cleaners a week.'

'Well, I just hope she lasts with us,' Holly said. 'I had to help Muv with the cleaning before she came and it's hopeless at our place. It's so big. When you get to the end you have to start all over again.'

Jake said, 'I don't think it's right, all those jobs you have to do. You need your freedom.'

'No. Suppose it isn't,' Holly said slowly. But she felt strangely torn. Muv and Farve *did* put upon her, rather. Yet she still felt loyal to them. They did such good things for people. As for 'freedom', what did Jake do with it? Nothing much, as far as she could see. He just wandered aimlessly about, skipped school, and sat in his room and smoked.

She said, 'Doris is good for Nan. They gossip. Muv calls her News of the World. Muv says if you want people to know your private business, tell Doris it's a secret . . . Doris's Handy Hints . . .' she said thoughtfully. 'She uses soot to get scratches off furniture, and she's shown me the proper way to iron a shirt. She learned that in a factory when she was fourteen.'

'Thought you didn't believe in things like ironing?' Jake said sharply. 'Thought you didn't believe in slaving for men, and getting married?'

'I don't. Perhaps we won't have Handy Hints then. Talking of slaving, I think you should brush that soil off the carpet. It'll tread in.'

'You sound like Laura,' sighed Jake, going to fetch a dustpan.

Jake had got two videos out from the shop. Perhaps that was where the ten pounds had gone. Holly settled down and watched them with him, and they were long. It was eleven o'clock when the second one finished. A magnificent grandfather clock in the hall was just chiming the hour as two lovers walked towards a lake into a fried-egg sunset.

Holly shot to her feet, panic washing over her like a great wave. *Eleven o'clock!* Even Farve would be back from his meetings. What if someone investigated the hump in her bed? What if Farve had been snooping? Her bones told her that trouble lay in store.

She borrowed Jake's bicycle lamp to light the path and pelted home along the canal. She knew it was dangerous, not just because of who might be hanging around down there, but because of the very real risk of slipping. But she was desperate. And as she let herself in through the back gate she knew that her bones had told her the truth. Through the side window she could see a terrifying little cameo, Muv and Farve sitting on either side of the gas fire, with the clock between them on the table, and next to the clock the telephone. Farve was going through her little address book, her personal one where she kept the phone numbers of her friends.

She burst in. 'I'm sorry.' Muv got up, gave her a hug and let out a shaky kind of sigh. Holly thought it was the sound of fighting back tears. Farve just sat there with her address book in his hand. The pink hedgehogs on the cover (it was another present from Fat Nan) looked particularly ridiculous. Farve himself looked very grim indeed, somehow

37

thinner than ever, black, tall and stooping like a giant rook. His dog-collar lay discarded on the table, his shirt was unbuttoned and she could see the fuzz on his chest. He looked as if he'd not had a good night's sleep in months.

He said, 'I've been going through this book of yours, to find out where you were. You are deceitful, Hannah, stuffing your bed with pillows. It was a great shock to your mother.'

When Farve got really angry with her he always talked about how *Muv* felt. His own feelings, it seemed, were too private. That was wrong, Holly thought, and it was why nobody could get close to him. He certainly *did* have feelings, about Fat Nan's illness, about his church, about Muv.

She said, 'My address book's private. And my room's private. Why do you have to go snooping?'

'Don't be impertinent.' His voice was icy cold. 'This is my house and in my house there are rules. I expect you to obey them.'

'I've only been with Jake Tolland. We were watching some videos, that's all. Is it a crime? Anyhow, isn't it OUR house? Don't I live in it as well?'

Farve ignored this. He said, 'The rule is that you don't go out without permission. And at your age you don't stay out till eleven o'clock at night.' He looked at the clock. 'Till eleven fifteen. It's outrageous.'

Holly said nothing. His reaction was so ridiculous. She felt she had absolutely nothing to say to him. So she just grunted, 'I'm going to bed.'

'Would you like some cocoa, pet?' Muv stood up, but Farve made her sit down again. 'You are *not* going to bed, Hannah. You are going to say you're sorry.'

Holly said fiercely, 'I'm *not* sorry. I've only done what everybody does at my age – gone to a friend's to watch the television and come home a bit late. Other people don't get 'permission', they just go. *You* go out. You're *always* going out.'

'I'm your father, Hannah. I have to go out, to do my work.'

Holly turned her face away. 'Goodnight, Muv.' She put her arms round her mother and snuggled in. Then she went off up the stairs, not looking back.

She could tell from the feel of the attic that Farve had been going through all her things. Perhaps he had even read her diary. Jake was right. If your parents gave you a room it was YOUR ROOM. If, like him, you turned it into a pigsty that was up to you. Her room was not a pigsty, it was the most orderly room at the vicarage. And Farve had overlooked one thing. The heavy arched

Victorian door had a large key — rusty, but a key that worked.

From now on she would lock her room up when she went out, and, from tomorrow morning, she would do what she liked. Farve was a tyrant and he had no right to lay down the law. He had no time for her. He didn't understand her. He was much too busy Doing Good. And Muv just got steam-rollered by him. Look how she'd obeyed him just now, not making the cocoa.

From now on she would live her own life. It was the holidays and that meant six weeks without school, so more Life than usual. If she went out she'd leave notes, like her parents did. She'd put the pig on the table and they could look in the Safe Place.

But what, exactly, was she going to *do* . . .? She was falling asleep now. Well, she didn't know, but she'd probably spend a lot of time with Jake. She might even go stealing, or run off and join some travellers, like Auntie Linda.

F i v e

Next day, when she woke up, Holly couldn't find her shoes. She looked everywhere, but she knew that she'd put them neatly side by side under her bedroom chair. She was a tidy person, a bit too tidy, perhaps. It was because the vicarage was always such a mess. She could at least control her own bit of it. But she longed to have a big airy room like Jake's. She could make it so lovely. There wasn't much hope in this dark, narrow attic.

She decided to put her slippers on and go downstairs. Someone had definitely moved her shoes, though she couldn't think why, unless Muv, in one of her very occasional 'blitzes', had gathered together all the shoes in the house and taken them to old Mr Woodward for mending. He was a retired cobbler and still mended shoes at home. He sang in the church choir. Yes, perhaps that was it.

Her slippers were missing too. They were not in the bottom of the wardrobe, on the left, where they lived. So she pulled on a pair of socks and padded downstairs in those. On the lower landing she met a man going into the bathroom. It wasn't hairy Cyril, the one who'd opened the loo door. This man was young and slender, with smooth fair hair done in a little ponytail. He had a smart navy towelling bathrobe and a Liberty sponge-bag. 'Hi,' he said. 'I'm Nathaniel.' His voice was plummy; it reminded her of the boys that went to St Wilfred's.

'I'm Holly,' she muttered, pushing past rather resentfully. 'I'm looking for my shoes.' She was thinking, how do you get to be a drop-in with a voice like that and a Liberty sponge-bag? Perhaps he wasn't a drop-in, perhaps he was a student, renting a room for honest cash. Whoever he was nobody had bothered to tell *her*. Farve'd be renting *her* room out next.

As she came into the kitchen she smelt cigarette smoke. She expected to see one of the drop-ins sitting at the table, but it was Doris. If the coast was clear and Muv and Farve were off the premises she liked a quick puff before she started cleaning.

Doris was tall and angular with a long lugubrious face. She wore her thin grey hair plaited and looped round her ears. It gave her the look of a very depressed sheep. Holly didn't know much about sheep, pigs were her preferred animal, but if Doris had been a sheep she'd definitely have been a depressed one.

She was quite lively though, in a gloomy kind of way. She talked a lot and knew exactly what was going on in all departments.

'You've not seen my shoes have you, Doris, or my slippers?' Holly put two pieces of bread in the toaster and filled the electric kettle.

'No, ducks. Sorry. I'll have a quick coffee, if you're making one. Then I'll do your nan's room. She's not in, I see. Gone out, have they?'

'I don't know. I expect they've left me a note.' Napoleon was on the table. Holly wasn't in a hurry to find out where Muv and Farve had gone off to. She was more bothered about her shoes.

There was a boot rack under the stairs. In this the family stored its footwear. There was a place for Holly's sneakers, for her wellingtons and for her school gym shoes. She opened the door and peered in. All the family shoes were there except hers. Where they should have been there were three gaps.

'No joy then, ducks?' Doris, sensing Holiday with No Rush, had lit a second cigarette.

'No. Absolutely all my shoes have disappeared.'

'Are you sure? That's a funny old business.'

'I'm positive. I think —' She looked at the pig.

43

Then, slowly, she started going through the various Safe Places.

'That Mrs Tolland's been up to her tricks again,' Doris said, blowing a smoke-ring. 'I did three hours for her the other day and she didn't leave my money out. I feel sorry for that boy. She neglects him, always gadding off, and the *men* . . . well, better not ask me about *them*. She's always shouting at him you know, always raising her voice. Poor lamb. She says he's too untidy. And I tell her, I know, I've had kiddies of my own. He's just going through a phrase. Ooh, she doesn't half shout though.'

'I know. It's her Daily Scream,' Holly said, coming out of the pantry with an envelope which she'd found tucked behind the tins. 'We're writing a newspaper about her. We're calling it the *Daily Scream.*'

Doris chortled. 'That's good. I like that. Better not tell your dad though.'

'No, I won't.' And don't you tell him, she wanted to say. Doris would probably tell Muv, and she wouldn't mind, but Farve hadn't got much sense of humour. He'd think it was disrespectful to parents.

'Where've they gone off to this time then, your mum and dad?' Holly could just hear her going on to Jake's mother. 'That Mr and Mrs Berry, it's shocking. Always going off and leaving that kiddy on her own.'

'Dad's only out till lunchtime and I've got to heat up a shepherd's pie for us. My mother's taken Nan to Blackpool. They've gone in Ethel's car. I suppose Ruthie's gone too.'

'Lovely lady, that Ethel. She was your nan's best friend you know, at school. They go back sixty years, those two. Why have you been left behind then, ducks?'

'Oh, I didn't want to go. I hate Blackpool.'

Holly was lying. She knew nothing at all about the trip. All she knew was what Farve had written in his note. She was 'gated' for the day, but he didn't trust her to obey him, not after last night. So he had taken away her shoes.

'Your dad's getting right steamed up about this festival he's having. Seen the safe in his study? Someone was throwing it away so he said he'd have it, just for the festival. Mind you, it's only a tiddly thing, not like the safes they had when I was in service . . . you hot, dear? You've gone a bit red in the face.'

'No, I'm not hot.' Over the kettle Holly wiped away a tear. She put her toast and her mug of tea on a tray and went off upstairs. On the landing she met Nathaniel again, all summery and smelling of tooth-paste. 'Cheer up,' he said, 'it might never happen.'

Holly scowled. Then she gritted her teeth. 'Listen,' she said, 'I don't know who you are and I don't suppose anyone's going to tell me. This is only my *home*. But if you say anything like that to me ever again I'll . . . I'll BRAIN YOU!'

The lovely Nathaniel stepped back. 'Beg your pardon,' he said. 'Pardon me for *living*.' And he disappeared into a bedroom in a cloud of lemon verbena soap.

Holly shut her bedroom door. Then she locked it. Then she took a gulp of tea and a bite of toast and honey. But she couldn't swallow it down. There was a big raw lump in her throat. She hated everybody in the world, but most of all she hated her father. She would NOT stay in. She would NOT make him shepherd's pie. And she would NOT leave a note in the Safe Place. She had moved Napoleon to guard one of the nappy buckets and that's where he was staying.

She pushed the breakfast tray away from her, threw herself on her lumpy bed and wept great hot tears. She had never been so unhappy.

When she had cried her cry she went into James's room and found a pair of his shoes. They were two sizes too big, but she put extra socks on. She locked her bedroom door and put the key in her pocket. Then she went downstairs.

Farve's 'personal timetable' was stuck up on the pin board. This was his morning for visiting the 'shut-ins', the people who were ill or very old and whom nobody went to see. Holly approved of these visits. She admired the way he always went and knocked on the door, even when people were rude to him. But if only, sometimes, he would speak to *her*. Didn't she matter too? She felt totally mixed up about him. It was as if, most of the time, he had to be on his best behaviour, because he was a vicar, but that he needed just one bit of his life where he could be himself, could storm about and get in tempers. That bit seemed reserved for Holly.

The shepherd's pie, lovingly made by Muv, sat on a shelf in the fridge. Someone had given them a microwave, so it shouldn't be beyond Farve to heat it up in that. Just for a minute she debated whether or not to throw it in the dustbin. But no. That would be too cheap, she decided. She left it where it was and shuffled across the road to St Bartholomew's church.

It was a very ugly building. They had only put it up a hundred years ago and it looked like a great big wedding-cake, all fancy bits and pieces squeezed out of stone and stuck on top, like icing. The stone was very dirty, because of all the traffic that roared past on the dual carriageway that ran along behind the graveyard. Not a quiet place to sleep when you were dead, thought Holly.

Inside, in a big glass case, were some chunks of masonry that had come from the original church. Now that *was* old, four hundred years old this month. That was why the festival was so important, why the bishop might come and why Farve had got a safe to put the gold plate in.

She went inside. The church used to be locked, because people stole things. Now everything worth money had been put away, the only thing left was a picture screwed to the wall. So far nobody had taken that. Anyhow, it wasn't valuable. It was just a little print of a great big picture in Russia, but it was Holly's favourite thing in the church. When she was grown up, and hadn't got married and become a doormat, she planned to visit Russia and see it for herself.

The picture was about the Prodigal Son, the boy in the Bible who said to his father, 'Give me my share of your money NOW,' the boy who went and spent it and ended up feeding the pigs. He was so hungry he tried to eat the pig food. Ugh. Then he decided to go home and he was so ashamed of himself he offered to become a servant, not be a proper son any more. But the father wasn't having that. He rushed out and gave the son a hug, then he threw a party for him. Everything was wonderful in the end, apart from the son's older brother. He was jealous. 'You never gave *me* a party,' he grumbled. 'And I've been a good son.' The father told him off, in a nice way. He said, 'Everything I've got belongs to you, but please be happy. Your "dead" brother is alive and well. It's marvellous.' Holly had always felt a bit sorry for that older brother.

She pulled up her favourite little blue mat from the Children's Corner and sat in front of the painting, hugging her knees. She'd first heard that story when she was little from Miss Spencer, the Sunday school teacher. One reason she liked it was because of the pigs, and the picture they'd been shown of the lost son sitting in the fields with them. She'd always been attached to pigs. In a way, the lost son must have ended up feeling a bit piggy himself, spending all his money on food and drink.

In this picture though, he looked really awful. You could only see his back. He was kneeling at his father's feet and he only had one shoe on. The other was all cracked and broken and there were great holes in his tunic. He had a round smooth head, like a baby's, and he was snuggling up to his father, burying his face in him. The father was a very old man. Holly could never decide what his face was saying to her. It was very gentle, but it was a bit stern too. It was ... *dignified*. You could tell he was a nobleman because he had a beautiful red cloak and gold bracelets. The lost son had a sword poking through his rags. He'd obviously not sold that.

The very best things were the old father's hands. They rested so gently on the shoulders of the baby-looking son, and the way the painter had got the light shining on them was brilliant. Rembrandt, the man who'd painted the picture, always did amazing things with light. Farve had told her that. In fact, it was Farve who'd told her all about the picture. How could Farve, who'd done that and spent all his time with drop-ins and shut-ins and being kind to people, have taken away her shoes? It was such a cruel thing to do. Holly looked at the painting in all its tenderness and cried again.

Then she heard someone opening the great big church door. It scraped the stone flags as it was pushed open. She dodged behind a pillar in the Children's Corner and watched as Farve, his black cassock over his arm, walked up to the front of the church and sat in the end of a pew.

He didn't do anything or say anything. She thought he might kneel down and say his prayers, but he just sat there. Might he be thinking about her, and the shoes? She could show herself. She could creep out and go and sit beside him. Perhaps they could talk, get close even.

No. Holly's heart hardened. He had hurt her feelings. He had *so* hurt them. And Muv must have gone along with him — unless she didn't know about the shoes. But Muv and Farve shared everything and made all their decisions together. Could they have quarrelled? Was that why he had come to sit in the church?

Very carefully, keeping to the shadows, she slipped out, leaving the door open. She wanted Farve to be like the father in the painting, a father that gave big hugs, someone that wasn't so . . . so *controlled* all the time. She supposed he *did* love them, her, James and N.O.P., but he felt so far-off most of the time. Why couldn't he just, well, *love* them?

She would go to Jake's. It was funny, Doris playing one family off against the other. Holly and Jake were in the same position. Her family had no money and his had a lot, but it didn't make any difference. Their parents were just the same in that they were all far too busy with grown-up things to look down and see what was going on under their noses.

Six

When she knocked on the door of 17, Addison Mews it was opened by Mrs Tolland. Holly, not expecting this, took a step back and stumbled. James's shoes were most definitely too big. Mrs Tolland peered down at her feet. 'I've come to see Jake,' Holly mumbled. 'Hope it's OK.'

Mrs Tolland did not, immediately, open the door any wider. She merely stood on the front doorstep, folded her arms, and stared with her glittery eyes. Holly felt that she was being inspected for cleanliness, possibly for infectious diseases.

Jake's mother was wearing navy-blue leggings and navy-blue shoes. On top she was wearing a long navy-blue Guernsey sweater, with the neatest of white collars folded over at the neck. 'She's Thinking Thin,' Holly thought expertly. 'And she's Dressing Dark.' She had 'Weight Watchers' written all over her. She was definitely too old for the leggings though. Holly was glad her mother didn't dress like that. 'Mutton dressed up as lamb' was how Doris had described Mrs Tolland.

She said, rather sourly, Holly thought, 'Well, I suppose so. He's in his room. He's tidying up. Actually he's going to go shopping for me in a little while.'

'It's all right. I wasn't going to stay very long.'

Mrs Tolland widened the gap in the door and Holly stepped inside. The hall carpet was, ridiculously, white. Jake's mother was cleaning it. A sponge and a soapy bucket sat under a radiator and half the floor was covered with foam. Without being asked, Holly took off James's sneakers and put them at the bottom of the stairs.

'Good girl,' clucked Mrs Tolland. She sounded just like the maths teacher at school. Slowly Holly made her way upstairs, scrunching her shoulders together and Thinking Thin.

Jake was half-heartedly dabbing at his floor-boards with a mop round which someone had tied a duster. 'I've got to wax it,' he said, 'when I've got the dirt off. *Honestly* . . .'

Holly sat on the bed. 'My father took my shoes away,' she said, and she burst into tears. Only now did she realize how very much she minded.

Jake was really nice to her. He sat on the bed beside her and patted her hand. Then he went to his wardrobe and brought out a big plastic carrier-bag. It was crammed with chocolate bars, every brand you could think of. 'Choose,' he said generously. 'Have whatever you like.' Holly, not wanting to think just how the chocolate had got there, took a king-sized Mars Bar. Jake, who had his own TV and computer up in his room, put on his favourite video, 'Children's TV Classics'. They watched peaceably together and got as far as the Flowerpot Men. Then Laura screamed up the stairs, 'Jacob ... JACOB! Have you finished your room yet? I need the shopping.'

Jake jerked to attention like a frightened whippet. 'Nearly. I'm just coming. Just finishing the floor.'

'Come on,' said Holly. They whizzed round for ten minutes. The bed was made, the ashtrays emptied into the black bin-liner provided, the tops dusted, all the clothes put into the wicker hamper that stood in the *en suite* bathroom. Holly even opened the windows. 'There you are,' she said. 'We've finished. The Queen could walk in here.'

Jake was full of admiration. 'That's brilliant.'

'Just practice,' Holly said rather sadly, thinking of all the rooms she'd tidied in her life, usually in preparation for one of the drop-ins.

'Got any further with the *Daily Scream*?' she said, as Jake pulled his shoes on.

'Not really. Have you?'

She smiled. 'Doris said you were "Going through

a phrase". I think she meant a *phase*, but I thought that was good. I thought, if we were going to have a thing about what parents say, you know, nagging, we could call it "Going Through a Phrase".'

'That's cool,' Jake said.

'And I thought I might do a story about Farve. I mean it could start, obviously, with him hiding my shoes. Then he might, er, tie me to the furniture, to stop me running away.'

Jake grabbed her arm. 'You don't think I'm serious about running away, do you?'

'Jacob? JACOB!' Mrs Tolland was getting impatient about her shopping.

'Hear that? Could you put up with that, day after day?'

'No, I couldn't. But then, would you like living in our house, people barging into the loo, and drop-ins all over the place, and nobody caring what you do all day, and your father taking away your shoes?'

'No, I wouldn't. We've both got problems. Run away with me. Serve them all right.'

'I couldn't. What about Muv?'

'What *about* her? You're always saying she's a doormat.'

'She is. I'm going to write Wipe Your Feet on her one of these days.'

*

55

They took a bus to the supermarket on the ring road. Mrs Tolland had insisted that this was where Jake was to do the shopping. She had given him a list and four five-pound notes. He was to bring the receipt back and she would check the change. Apart from the bus fare he was allowed to keep fifty pence for himself.

'Two steaks', read Holly. 'Iceberg lettuce . . . a RIPE avocado pear (if not ripe buy two grapefruit).' She said, 'Is this a dinner party?'

'Yes. Daniel's coming.'

'Why aren't you invited?'

He shrugged. 'Well, you know, it's not for the likes of me, is it? She thinks I'm a contagious disease.' Holly thought of Mrs Tolland's look when she opened the front door and said nothing. 'There's a pizza in the freezer for me,' he said. 'I'm permitted to eat it in my room.'

They reached the supermarket and went three times round inside the enormous glass swing doors. A smell of warm bread met them and Holly looked hungrily at the café and its advert for 'Coffee 'n' Danish, 99p'. She was getting angrier and angrier with Laura Tolland, and her own parents were beginning to sicken her too, the way they sent you away out of sight when anything important or interesting was happening, as if you were a kind of bad smell.

'It won't take me long to get these,' Jake said. 'You hang on here.'

She nearly said, 'Can't I come with you?' But she had a strong feeling that he wanted to be on his own, so she stayed near the checkouts and looked at the books. Supermarkets sold baby books now. If only she could buy one for N.O.P. She loved chewing books. But Holly didn't get pocket-money. If she really needed something it was bought for her, otherwise she was supposed to ask. And nobody liked asking. It was a ridiculous system, not a 'system' at all. MONEY. It could be another item in the *Daily Scream*. Parents had such queer ideas about it.

Jake was soon at the checkout. Out he came with two carrier bags. 'Now,' he said, 'we'll have a drink and a Danish.' And he headed for the café.

'But we've got no money.'

'I have.'

'But where —'

'Don't be nosy.'

Jake paid for the drinks and food from a bundle of new five-pound notes. They looked like the ones that came from the machine-in-the-wall. She'd once seen Farve get money out of one of those.

'Have you got your own bank account?'

'Course not. Come on. There's a bus in five minutes.'

They trundled into town. Every time she asked about the money Jake started whistling. In the end she said angrily, 'Listen, that's getting on my nerves.'

'Well, stop asking *questions* then. I had a right to that money. I'm getting off here. These are for you.'

From the carrier-bags he pulled something wrapped in another bag, dumped it in her lap and got off the bus. 'See you.'

Holly stared at the package as the bus jolted towards Museum Road, felt it, smelt inside. When they reached her stop she stayed on. She got off further along, at Tulliver Street, so she could walk back home along the canal. She wanted to think.

Jake's present was a pair of rainbow-coloured sneakers, her size. He had some too and she'd always said they were gorgeous. But how had he bought them? Were those new five-pound notes really his own money? Or was it stolen? Or were the sneakers stolen?

She sat on a bench and took off James's beaten-up shoes, pulling on the new ones. Her feet went in smoothly, like silk. Then she walked slowly along the towpath, carefully avoiding the puddles.

Ethel's Fiesta was parked outside the vicarage and N.O.P's buggy was by the front door. They were back from Blackpool already. She could hear

58

Farve laughing in the hall. *Laughing,* on the day he had stolen all her shoes.

That decided it. She pushed open the front door and walked in wearing her rainbow sneakers. They would ask questions and she would answer. It would be the truth but not, necessarily, the *whole* truth. Jake was her friend and he'd been kind to her. She wasn't going to get him into trouble.

However you looked at it though, given Farve and his way of looking at things, Holly felt it was WAR.

S e v e n

The minute he saw her Farve looked down at her feet. 'Where did you get those from, Holly?'

'Someone gave them to me. They were a present.'

'From whom?'

Holly just stood there. She wasn't going to tell.

'From *whom*, Holly?'

'Oh, just someone.'

'I think you should tell me.'

She took a very deep breath and walked past him, towards the stairs. 'And I think you should mind your own business,' she said, over her shoulder.

The silence was terrible. Nan was there, leaning on Ethel who, anticipating a family row, started nudging her towards her bedroom door.

'Go to your room, Holly,' ordered Farve.

'I'm going. AND THERE WAS NO REASON TO TAKE AWAY MY SHOES.' There. She'd said it, and without crying. She hated him.

Muv looked from one to the other in disbelief. 'William, you didn't. Oh, *William* . . . what did you have to do a thing like that for?'

Farve turned on his heel. 'I don't propose to discuss it. I have notes to write, for tonight's meeting. I think the Sinclairs may well be coming, by the way. That's another thing we'll have to sort out.' He went into his study and shut the door, leaving Muv and Holly staring at one another.

Holly didn't go up to her room. She followed Muv's frantic sign language and they went into the kitchen for a cup of tea. For the first time she admitted to herself what she thought she'd always known, that Muv was rather frightened of Farve and his strange moods.

Mrs Berry said, filling the kettle, 'I'm sorry, chicken. It was a very peculiar thing to do. But he's under great stress.'

'Perhaps it's in the Bible,' Holly said stonily, thinking how feeble Muv was and how she should have stuck up for her more, against Farve. 'Perhaps taking shoes away was a punishment from God.'

'No, I don't *think* so, pet. Removing your shoes was part of worship, of course —'

'Oh, *Muv*.' Holly was in no mood for a lecture.

'I'm afraid your father's got an awful lot on his mind. There's this festival coming up — and your nan's not at all well. She felt very faint in the car, that's why we came back early. Then there's the Sinclairs. They're another problem. Actually, I want to talk to you about them.'

'Why? Who are they?'

'A very needy family, a young couple and a baby. I think there's a toddler too. They're going to be homeless in a few days.'

'And they're moving in with us?'

'Well, they might have to, just for a bit.'

'OK,' said Holly, thinking, So what's new?

'The thing is, there are four of them. The best place would be the top of the house, with the kitchenette handy and everything. James'll be away for three weeks so *his* room's available and —'

'NO.'

'Now don't say that, pet. It wouldn't be permanent. It'd just be for a few days. We thought you could have the little room next to Nan's bathroom.'

'We.' That meant it had already been discussed with Farve. Now she was going to have her attic room taken away so it could be occupied by this problem family and she was being shoved into the damp little boxroom where they stored the suitcases. Her shoes were probably in there at this very moment. It was one of her father's Safe Places. On the way down to her new premises she would most probably meet Nathaniel waving his flowery

62

sponge-bag, hairy Cyril and no doubt dozens of others to whom her parents had offered a welcome. She was living in a madhouse.

'I don't think I want any tea,' she said.

'Let me help you find your shoes, lovie. Oh dear, that really was such a hair-brained thing to do, hiding your shoes. I'm sorry, love.'

'Pea-brained', said Holly under her breath. 'It's all right. I expect they're in my new bedroom.' And she went to look among the suitcases. She had made a decision. If the Sinclairs or anybody else came to live in her attic without her permission she would move out. There were people at school with whom she sometimes stayed overnight. There was Rachel, there was Elizabeth, and if they couldn't have her there was always Jake. He spent so much time on his own he'd be glad of the company.

She decided to go and see him, but before she went she assembled all her shoes together and took them upstairs. Then she put her old trainers on and placed the rainbow shoes side by side in the old trunk that lived under her bed. Underneath them she put her address book and her diary. Then she examined the trunk. It was very old and dented and the hasp was rusty, but it definitely could be locked. All she needed was a padlock.

She would ask Jake to get her one. He had plenty of money. He seemed able to get anything. Probably most of his stuff was stolen. Well, so what? If Jake was leading her into bad ways whose fault was it? It was Muv's, partly, for being so feeble and never sticking up for herself, and it was Farve's, Farve's for snooping, and for doing cruel things.

Jake wasn't very interested in what had happened at the vicarage. 'Oh yeah,' he kept saying in a flat, dead voice. He was smoking furiously.

'What's up?'

'Nothing,' he scowled.

'Yes there is. Something's upset you.'

At first he wouldn't tell; then, in a rush, it all came out. 'My mother's really keen on this Daniel bloke. She's saying she might marry him now.'

'Might? Doesn't she know?'

Jake wiggled his shoulders and gulped hard. 'Well, she says she's thinking about it. He's asked her.'

Holly said, 'Would it make all that much difference? I mean, she's had loads of boyfriends, hasn't she?'

'Yeah, but getting married . . . that's never come into it before.'

He stared at his feet. New shoes again, Holly

noticed; expensive trainers this time. Where had he nicked those from, she wondered. Not from that supermarket. They were too high class.

He said, 'I'd quite like to see my dad.'

'Why can't you?'

'Because he lives in Spain, in this villa. The woman he married, she's just had a baby. They don't want me around. I might be going, not till next summer though.' His mouth trembled. 'I don't like it where they are, in Spain. It's too hot. It made me ill, the time I went. And it's boring. There's nothing to do there apart from swimming. People just sit round.'

'Well, swimming's OK,' Holly said gently. 'I wouldn't mind it. We never go anywhere. And I bet your dad would like you to see the baby. I mean it's yours too, sort of.'

Jake wasn't listening. 'Before he went to Spain we had this barn, up north. It was right out in the wilds, it was brilliant. My mum and dad, they were trying to turn it into a house. There was a stream. It went right past the door, ooh, and the hills, there were hills all round. It was fabulous. Wish I could go back there.'

'Why don't you? Why don't you and your mum go back?'

'Because they sold it, that's why. But that's where I'm going, when I run away. You don't need an air ticket to go there. You can just get on to the motorway. Nobody'll nag and scream at me there.'

His voice was tight with a fierce, explosive passion and, for a while, there was silence. Then Holly, for something to say, muttered, 'Done anything to the *Daily Scream*?'

'Not really. But Doris says you can clean carpets with tea-leaves. That might come in useful. My mother's having a blitz on her carpets. Everywhere you walk it's wet. I think I'm getting pneumonia.'

Holly smiled. 'I think this newspaper's not got what it takes, do you? I mean, News Flash: WOMAN CLEANS CARPET WITH TEA-LEAVES. It doesn't sound like a world headline, does it?'

'How about 'Vicar Steals Shoes'?' Jake said slyly. 'Is that any better?'

To her surprise, Holly found that she didn't like this attack on Farve. It was all right for *her* to say things about him, but not for Jake.

She said defensively, 'Muv didn't know what he'd done. Well, how could she? She says he's got too much to worry about. He goes on and on about this festival though. He's talking of getting a burglar alarm rigged up now.'

'Isn't there one already?'

'No. There's nothing to steal, not where we live.

But he's getting this gold plate out of the bank, to use at the festival.'

'I know. Doris told me.'

Holly grew thoughtful. So News of the World had been gossiping again. She hoped her father didn't find out. He'd ask Doris to leave and Muv needed her help, even though she did smoke and was the dirtying lady.

Jake said, 'I could fix up an alarm for your father. It wouldn't cost him anything if I did it. Why don't we go and have a look at the site?'

'"The site ..."' Holly said uncertainly. It sounded very official, as if Jake was planning a robbery and had been working out his strategy.

'Where this gold plate's going to go. You *know*. Don't be thick.'

'Oh no, we can't. The church'll be locked up,' Holly said hurriedly.

This wasn't true. One of Farve's things was that his church stood open, for anybody who wanted to go there. But she felt distinctly uncomfortable to hear Jake asking so many questions about the burglar arrangements. Nicking chocolate bars and shoes was bad enough but the St Bartholomew gold plate ... Surely Jake couldn't be planning anything to do with *that*. If he was, though, she knew one thing: angry as she was with Farve, she wanted absolutely nothing whatsoever to do with it.

Eight

Jake was restless. He didn't want to stay in his room any more. He'd heard his mother come in with Daniel. Sexy music was now floating up from the drawing-room and squeezing its way under his door. He looked in pain.

'Let's go to your place,' he mumbled.

'No. My father's at home. He's working in his study and I don't want to speak to him. Anyhow, if my mother sees me she'll make me look after Ruthie.' Since Fat Nan had come to live with them Holly had had to do a lot more baby-minding. She loved N.O.P., but not when she had one of her prolonged grizzles, and nowadays these always seemed to start the second Muv had turned her back.

They decided to go shopping, not to buy any-thing, just to look. Jake seemed quite cheered up by the prospect. A tiny bit of Holly felt excited. What if Jake pinched something and she saw him?

Wouldn't that mean she was involved in a crime? She knew that, really, she ought to refuse point blank to go round the shops with him, but she couldn't resist. The truth was, she felt bored. Sometimes people became murderers out of boredom, didn't they? So what was to stop people thieving out of boredom?

Jake didn't quite fit into this though. Holly's theory was that he stole things because his mother spent most of her time out of the House — or making sure that *he* kept out of the House, in case he dirtied it. 'He's an Only,' she'd told Muv and Farve, when she'd met them at a Parents' Night. But 'Only' meant 'Lonely' to Holly. She was glad she'd got N.O.P. and James, even if he was away at school. Muv cared about her a lot. So did Farve, deep down, even in his shoe-hiding mode. They were a proper family. Jake had nobody. That was why he went thieving.

He seemed anxious to window-shop in the great big stationer's that had opened on the industrial site at the end of Museum Road. It was huge, an old warehouse stuffed full of anything you could possibly need to furnish a super deluxe office. They had computers that you could play on, and desk chairs that swirled round and round. They had toys too, and sweets, bits of everything really. It was called 'Aladdin's'.

Holly insisted on their walking past St Bartholomew's to avoid the front of the vicarage. The church door was open. Jake noticed at once. 'Thought you said your dad kept the door locked?'

'He does, sometimes, only . . .' Holly's voice petered out weakly.

'Ugh, I hate that.' And Jake pointed.

'So do my parents.' 'That' was the large wooden crucifix which hung outside the church on a bit of scrubby ground where people threw chip papers and let their dogs make a mess. People had strong feelings about the statue because it was very, very big. Farve had always wanted it removed but there was some old document that said he couldn't. It was all to do with the land the church had been built on.

Holly, though she had never told anyone this, quite liked it because, although the Jesus figure was very big and horribly blackened by traffic fumes, the actual face was smiling. Sometimes she dreamed about that smiling face. She liked it better than the idea of God, who felt to her so cross and full of rules and regulations, always out to snoop on you. God was all mixed up with Farve these days, she couldn't sort him out at all.

Before she could stop him Jake had slipped inside the church, so she had to go too. Not that there was anything to steal, but somehow, knowing

70

Jake was inside, made it *her* church, on behalf of Farve, and she felt an unexpected rush of loyalty to him, a feeling that was suspiciously like love.

'Smells funny,' was Jake's opening gambit as he wandered round.

'I like it,' Holly said. It was just 'Church' to her; mustiness and old books, the smell you get after a candle is snuffed out, flowers – there were always flowers in St Bartholomew's and now, in summer, people brought lots, from their gardens. Muv helped do the arrangements with Miss Sparrow and Mrs Teale. They were the Flower Ladies. Mr Prestbury, an old, old man, looked after the Children's Corner. He cleaned the blue carpet and the little mats the children sat on. He sorted out their books and toys. Everyone had a job to do. People cared about this place, even though only a few came to the services.

Once Holly had loved it, the high pointed windows full of technicoloured saints wreathed round with leaves and sheep and eagles, the organ with its gold-painted pipes, the blue-robed choir ladies in their funny square hats. The old ones wobbled a bit when they soared up high, but she'd still loved the music. The best moment was when they processed in after Farve, following the big brass cross that was held so high. 'This is God, now,' she'd once whispered to Muv, when she was little. 'This is God.'

But it didn't feel so comforting any more. It was because of the sad things, because of people like Jake and all those people in her class whose mums and dads were getting divorced, because of the people who fell ill, like Fat Nan, just when she should be enjoying her life, up in the little Scottish cottage with Thin Gramps, Thin Gramps who'd suddenly died in his chair. Fat Nan really upset her, sitting there day after day, helpless, more helpless than N.O.P. She decided that it was mainly because of Fat Nan that she'd gone off God.

Jake was staring at the picture of the father and the son. 'I like that,' he said.

Holly was pleased. 'So do I. Look at his poor feet. He's only got one shoe on.'

'He looks like a skinhead. He's not got any hair. He's like your baby. "And he fain would fill his belly with the husks that the swine did eat,"' he muttered to himself.

Holly was amazed. 'That's the Bible. That's what it says, about him eating the pig food.'

'I know.'

'*How* do you know? And how do you know the old-fashioned words?'

Jake shrugged. 'Just do. S'pose I learned it at St Wilf's. There was a lot of religion there. It's crap, I think.'

Holly, not sure any more whether God was

'crap' or not, followed him up to the front of the church. The table below the great East window was empty, apart from two old candlesticks. They were only pottery. The silver ones were in the bank.

Jake stared up and down. 'Is this where the burglar system is going to go then, up here?'

Holly felt a little stab of fear. 'I don't know.'

'Well, this is where your father will be, isn't it, you know, doing his thing with the wine and bread?'

'Yes, but —'

'I bet I could nick things from here. Even if he did rig a system up. You can cut through them, you know.'

Holly stared at him, simply not knowing whether he was joking or off in some strange fantasy world where young boys hit vicars on the head and ran away with priceless treasures.

She said very deliberately, 'So when my father gets the gold plate out of the bank you're going to come in here and steal it? Then what will you do?'

Jake turned pink. 'Dunno. Pawn it. It'd fetch enough for us to run away.'

'We're not *going* to run away.'

'I am. I'll go on my own. I don't care. Just let her do one more thing to me, that's all. She treats me like . . . like dirt.'

Holly said, 'Listen. She's unhappy. She wants to marry Daniel and she feels guilty, because of you. She does love you, she's just, well, unhappy.'

'Everyone's unhappy,' Jake said bleakly.

'Let's go to Aladdin's,' she suggested. Shopping was the only thing that cheered him up at the moment, and perhaps, this time, he wouldn't take anything.

He followed her out of the church and round to the main road again, past the big looming Jesus, smiling on his cross. They'd just got to the gate of the graveyard when Holly heard Muv's voice. 'Holly . . . thank goodness. Can you come and give me a hand? I don't know where your father's got to. Is that Jake? Jake, chicken, can you come too? We need a strong man.'

They waited for a break in the traffic then crossed the road together.

'It's your nan,' Muv said, hurrying them inside. 'Doris and I have been struggling for half an hour. She's stuck in the bath. She's stuck to the bottom. We need all hands on deck. I *do* wish I could get hold of your father . . .'

Nine

They followed Muv along the hall and into the little bathroom next to Fat Nan's room. It was extremely hot and steamy, and they couldn't see properly. This was just as well. Holly really didn't want to see her grandmother sitting in the bath and she was sure Jake didn't.

Muv went straight in while they hovered by the door. Doris was bent over the bathtub, her long stringy arms heaving and straining. 'If you could just get a better grip, lovie . . .'

But Nan was whimpering, 'I can't. It's the pain. And I've no strength in my arms. I think you'll have to get help, Mary.' This was to Muv, who had taken up a tugging position at the other end of the tub.

Jake, from the doorway, whispered to Holly, 'If the bathmat's really stuck, the thing is to break the suction, get something underneath it.'

'But Nan's so heavy,' Holly whispered back. 'I

don't think they can move her to get at the mat, that's the trouble.'

'These silly mats,' Doris was saying. 'Should never have been invented if you ask me. You need a nice modern non-slip bath, Granny.' Doris had an irritating habit of spending other people's money for them, and yet it was perfectly obvious that the vicarage family didn't have any.

'Heave ho,' said Muv cheerfully, but with a faint desperation in her voice. Through the steam, from their post at the door, Holly and Jake saw what looked like a baby whale wobble and splash, make a tiny heaving motion, then, with a groan, sink back beneath the bubbles again.

'Let's empty the bath,' Doris said decisively, and she pulled the plug out.

'But Nan'll get cold if you do that,' Holly pointed out. She was feeling really sorry for her grand-mother now, exposed like that in the bathtub, with everybody looking on. Not that she and Jake *were* looking. They really were *not*. Nan's helplessness reminded Holly of N.O.P. It was a done-to life, being a baby, and when you grew old it was a done-to life all over again. You couldn't do things for yourself, any more than a baby could. Others had to take care of you and, in the end, you just had to do as you were told. It all made her want to cry, somehow.

Suddenly, News-of-the-World Doris gave a little squeak of triumph. There was rather a rude plopping, sucking kind of noise and Fat Nan got shakily to her feet, just as the last of the bathwater swirled down the plughole.

Jake disappeared and Holly heard the front door slam. She went into the bathroom where Muv and Doris were now swaddling Nan in a fluffy pink towel and helped swaddle too. 'Thank you, dear,' Fat Nan said breathily. Her face was a funny colour, not red and boiled as it usually is when you've just had a bath, but a greenish-grey. She looked ill. Farve was worried about her. Muv had said so.

'Please don't let Nan die,' Holly said silently, in spite of the muddle she felt about God.

Jake didn't come back till Nan was tucked up in bed talking to the Health Visitor. Holly was in the kitchen with Muv and N.O.P. Farve was nowhere in sight. He put a carrier-bag on the table. 'Aladdin's', it said in green and gold. 'These are for your granny,' Jake mumbled. 'Sorry they're not wrapped up.'

Holly peeped inside and saw a gigantic box of chocolates done up in fancy ribbon.

'The receipt's in the bag,' he said under his breath. 'And it was *my money*.'

'That was very, very sweet of you, dear,' Muv

said, and she gave him a kiss. Muv didn't just peck people, she gave them big warm hugs.

Holly looked nervously at Jake. Did he mind being swamped, covered with comfy feathers by hen-like Muv? She had never seen his own mother touch him, let alone give him a kiss.

'Well, it was awful for her,' Jake said awkwardly, 'us being there, and everything. I didn't *look*,' he added.

'Of course you didn't, love, and she's going to be absolutely delighted with her present. All right, all *right*, precious petal ...' N.O.P. was grizzling and extremely smelly. Muv took her out of her high chair and bore her away upstairs.

'I didn't nick those chocolates,' he said.

Holly looked at him.

'I didn't, I'm telling you.'

'OK, *OK*. I believe you.'

He stared round the kitchen and his eyes rested on Farve's pin-board. It was a model of neatness, four drawing-pins to each notice and everything arranged with mathematical precision. There were different sections, 'monthly', 'weekly' and 'daily'; the word that came up most often was 'jobs'. Even Fat Nan had a job it seemed, something to do with sorting out the vicarage newspapers and putting cuttings into folders. Holly had endless jobs, monthly, weekly and daily; dustbins to carry out and shoes to clean – not just her own either, but other people's, or so it seemed to Jake. There were a lot of extremely boring things on the list, the washing of jam-jars for the summer fête, sorting out old clothes for jumble sales and even sewing buttons on. He was amazed. Why did Holly *do* all this? She was always saying that being a baby was what she called a 'done-to' life. *Hers* was a done-to life, if ever there was one.

Holly wasn't like any other girl he knew. She was much more grown up. That was why he felt safe with her. But she was a bit too serious. It was all these jobs she had to do. They were making her old before her time.

In their own way her parents were as bad as his mother, worse really. At least he had time to himself. All that baby-minding as well. Jake didn't really like babies, the smell and the mess. One reason he didn't want to go to Spain to see his father was the new baby. Then he remembered something.

'I got this for your Ruthie,' he said, digging into his pocket.

Cautiously, Holly stretched out a hand. It was a small brown teddy bear, with a red ribbon round its neck, a tiny knitted ski-hat and tiny knitted boots. 'It's lovely,' she said slowly.

'D'you think she'll like it?'

79

'Well, yes. Mind you, she'll eat it. It'll have to go on a shelf for a bit. Did you buy this too, from Aladdin's?'

Jake's eyes slid away. The little bear had fitted so perfectly into his pocket. Anyhow, those chocolates had been really expensive, and that *was* his money, well, money he had a right to.

Holly had tightened her mouth and was obviously going to start the Inquisition when her father walked in.

'Where's your mother? She rang me about Nan. What are you doing here?' This was to Jake.

Jake shot to his feet. 'Nothing. I mean, I was just going. Bye, Holl.' And he was gone.

Holly glared at her father as the back door was pulled shut. 'Why did you have to do that? He wasn't doing any harm.' She wanted to say, ' A wonderful Christian *you* are.' She would, one of these days.

Her father ignored her. Then he said, '*Holl* . . . I don't like him calling you that. Why can't he use your proper name?'

'Holly's not my proper name either, actually.'

He snorted. 'You are *impossible*.'

'Jake's been really good. He helped get Nan out of the bath.' This wasn't exactly what had happened, but he'd come with her, and he'd only not gone into the bathroom because it was embarrassing. You couldn't blame him for that. He'd never, ever called her 'Holl' before, though. She had warmed to it. It meant he really liked her.

'What do you mean? What on earth was your grandmother doing in her bath with – with that boy there?'

'She got stuck to the bottom. She couldn't get out. Muv said we all had to pull, but in the end she and Doris managed between them. The Health Visitor's come. I think Nan's a bit shaky.'

The minute she mentioned Nan her father walked out of the kitchen, only pausing to say, as if it were the most natural development in the world, 'Oh, the Sinclairs are definitely coming, by the way. We'll need your room.'

Holly sat on at the kitchen table, clutching the little brown bear against her chest. She had hidden it from Farve, in case he asked questions. Slowly, with a certain weariness, she looked round at the shabby room, the faded paint, the greasy cooker (Doris didn't 'do' cookers), the old-fashioned airing rack full of shirts (she didn't always 'do' ironing either). The house was full. Nathaniel was still on the first floor and there were two young girls sharing the back bedroom, who clumped about at night and played a radio loudly. They'd been sent from the Centre for a few days. They seemed homeless too.

She got up, left the kitchen and started to climb the stairs. Inside her a resolution was hardening. If the Sinclairs did come, and if she really *did* have to leave her room, then she was leaving, for Rachel's or for Elizabeth's, for Jake's, anywhere. She might even join him on his pilgrimage to this old barn in the hills, though she knew, deep down, that going there could only be a dream.

She unlocked her bedroom, went in and locked it again. Then she pulled out the old trunk from under the bed. On top of the rainbow-coloured shoes she carefully placed Little Bear. That was what she would call him.

She knew he was stolen. Jake's slithery eyes had told her that. And now he wasn't going to be given to N.O.P., so that was another kind of stealing. But she loved him. She would take him with her on her journey, wherever it led her. Carefully, she closed the lid on him, feeling suddenly rather grown up and, unexpectedly, filled with a kind of peace.

T e n

That Friday (Holly always remembered the day. It went down in her memory as Bad Friday) several things happened at once. Nothing was supposed to happen except that she was going off for the weekend with the Guides, and on the Sunday Farve was holding his Patronal Festival, the day of their saint, St Bartholomew.

He had been grumpy all week because the bishop, having promised he'd come, then rang to say he couldn't. Some important person had died and he had to conduct a service. It was going to be on telly. 'Typical,' Farve had snorted. 'He's all high profile, that man.'

Holly didn't understand. Muv explained rather hesitantly that the bishop was a little bit of a snob, that he probably wouldn't think Farve's festival worth missing a TV appearance for. 'A dear man, but he does have his problems,' she'd said vaguely. This meant she didn't like him at all.

Doris got into trouble on Bad Friday too. Farve had to get the gold plate from the bank and put it into his new safe. He didn't know how to transport it from the High Street to Museum Road. He was worried that if he used his car or got a taxi they might break down and he'd be sitting there clutching the thing, just asking to be mugged. If he walked someone might pounce and run off with it. There wasn't enough money to use a security firm, so in the end he used his bicycle. He'd always said you were 'your own master' on a bike, first away at the traffic-lights, always able to squeeze past in tight situations. So he put on his helmet and his fluorescent chest-bands and pedalled off.

Holly felt quite excited, because he'd told her that she could see the plate before he put it in the safe. But she never did get to see it. As he wheeled his bicycle into the drive, on his way back from the bank, two men appeared, one with a camera and one with a notebook. They were from the *Darnley Examiner*, a newspaper Farve detested because it had so many spelling mistakes and always got the facts wrong about happenings at St Bartholomew's. 'About this relic you've got, vicar, a little bird told me it was worth fifty thousand . . .' the one with the notebook began, licking his pencil.

Farve pushed past him and marched into the house with his padded envelope from the bank, threatening to call the police if the men didn't go away. Then he started to interrogate Holly. Had she told anyone about the gold plate and what it was worth? No, she said, and No. Well, she'd no idea what it was worth but she *had* told Jake. She lied about that bit because she was frightened of what her father might do to him if she confessed. There'd been all those questions about the burglar alarm. He rang Jake up anyway, but he wasn't there. Holly could hear Farve being very curt and brisk with Mrs Tolland. He was dead sure it was Jake.

But it wasn't. It was gossip Doris. She'd told her neighbour Freda about the gold plate, and Freda had told her Jack, and Jack had talked about it that night, down in the pub. It was Muv who pieced together how the story got out.

'She'll have to go,' Farve stormed, locking the padded envelope up in the safe without showing the plate to anyone. 'She's a troublemaker.'

But Muv defended Doris. 'Everyone's interested in a thing like that, pet,' she said. 'And Doris wouldn't think she was doing any harm. She's a good woman. She's so patient with your mother, and marvellous with the children. I can't do *every-thing* myself.'

But Farve was firm. 'At the end of the month she can go. We'll all have to pull our weight a bit more round here, that's all.' Holly's heart dropped into her boots. She couldn't see how any more jobs could be squeezed into her 'personal' diary. She wanted to point out that the way to cut down on the housework was to be a normal family, just Muv and Farve, Holly, James and N.O.P., to get rid of all the drop-ins and the hangers-on.

'Can I see the plate?' Holly said.

'No you canNOT.'

Nobody ever did get to see it. It was stolen, before the festival happened. But Holly only found that out later. AFTERWARDS as she always called it, the biggest AFTERWARDS that had ever happened to her.

She was supposed to be packing for Guide camp. She had a kit list and she was depressed because she didn't have half the things. Rachel, whose house she might be sleeping in that night, because it was an early start next day, had said it was OK, they had loads of sleeping-bags and things like that. She could borrow a windcheater and a hat too. Holly just wished she could take her *own* things. Muv had told her to go through the jumble boxes, but she didn't want to. She was sick and tired of wearing the clothes that other people had chucked out.

Someone knocked on her door. It was Muv to

say that Jake was on the phone. 'He seems rather agitated, chickie,' she said. 'Nice boy. Sensitive. Take it in our room.'

Holly, glad that someone in the family, apart from her, approved of Jake, climbed on to her parents' creaking brass bed, curled up and answered the phone. The room was a mess. Its main features were stacks of black plastic sacks full of useful items that Muv was always on the point of 'sorting out', and piles and piles of books, nearly all belonging to Farve, books with curious titles like *Doubt and Reason* and *Light in Darkness*. She would write a book when she was grown up, she decided, a book about this room, and present it to Muv and Farve. She would call it *Order out of Chaos* or possibly *Neatness from Squalor*.

She grinned as she picked up the handset. But Jake was in no mood for jokes. 'She's had it,' he said. His voice was half a snarl and half a sob. There was a long pause after he said, 'She's had it,' then a funny snuffling noise. Holly knew he was crying.

'What happened, Jake?'

'I spilt a cup of coffee, on the white carpet. I was carrying it upstairs and I tripped. She wasn't in, so I got some carpet shampoo and tried to get rid of it, but it just made it worse. It sort of . . . spread, you know. Anyhow, I thought I'd try tea-leaves, like Doris told us. I made the tea —'

Holly gasped. 'You MADE tea . . . you mean you used it fresh, on the white carpet?'

'Well, yes. Isn't that what you're supposed to do?'

She hesitated. 'I'm . . . I'm not sure. I thought perhaps you had to dry them first. I think they're just for getting the dust up.'

'The point is that I've ruined her carpet. The tea-leaves made it worse. It looks horrible. I could kill Doris. Silly cow.'

Poor Doris, both a sheep and a cow. Holly had a vision of her mooing over a large teapot, and smoking one of her drooping fags.

'I've packed anyway. I'm going.'

'You're not.'

'Yes I am. She hit me. She was cruel. Coming with me?'

'No. I mean I can't. I'm going to camp.'

'Come with me instead. I'm going to our barn. You can camp in that. At least you won't have to put a silly tent up each night.'

'No, honestly, I can't. And listen, you can't either. People don't just run away.'

'They do, every day. I've told you, I've packed. I've worked out the money and everything.'

At that moment Farve came into the room and

Holly jumped off the bed. 'Muv told me to speak on this phone,' she stammered. 'She gave me permission. Listen,' she said to Jake, 'I'll see you. Got to go now.'

'Phone me if you change your mind,' he said, and rang off.

'Who was that?' Farve said.

'Jake.'

He scowled. 'I need to talk to you, Holly.' She knew that tone of voice. It meant it was Desperately Important, to Farve, not necessarily to her. It was almost certainly about the Sinclairs.

She said, 'I've got to go to the Guide hut. There's a meeting, about tomorrow.'

He looked annoyed, but he said, 'Oh, I see. Well, I suppose you can't miss that. I must say it's a pity you're away the weekend of the festival.'

'I didn't plan it.'

'There's no need to be rude.'

She'd not meant it to sound like that, but a great anger about Farve was mounting inside her. It was never, 'How are things going, Holly?' or 'How are *you*, Holly?' It was always, 'Do this,' 'Do that,' or, 'I need to talk to you.' She felt she wasn't a person to her father, merely an extension of his endless 'arrangements'. Most deeply she felt that all the needy people who came to the vicarage were just as important as she was. And she wanted to be more important. She wanted to be special and needed for herself, not just because she was useful.

The meeting at the Guide hut took ages. Mrs Beresford, the Guider, did go on. She took ten sentences to say what anybody else would have said in one. Holly was glad it was only a weekend and not a week. Afterwards she went to Rachel's to collect a sleeping-bag and a windcheater. Rachel, who was an Only, like Jake, pressed her once again to stay the night, so that they could set off together next morning.

'I'd have to ask,' Holly said. 'My father doesn't much like it when I stay at other people's houses.'

'Why not?'

'Oh, he gets anxious. I'm sorry. He's just a bit odd about it. Anyhow, I'll ring if he says yes.'

But she didn't go to Rachel's. Nor did she go to camp. When she got back to the vicarage she went straight up to her room with the sleeping-bag. The door was open, even though she'd locked it. Farve, of course, had his own keys for every door in the house.

A young woman was sitting on her bed, giving a baby its bottle. She was smoking. From time to time she flicked ash on to the bedside rug. Some of it settled on the baby. In a corner was a small TV set. It was on, showing an old *Pink Panther* cartoon. 'Reception's not much cop up here,' she said, looking rather resentfully at Holly. 'Don't you have a proper aerial?'

'No. I'm not allowed television in my bedroom,' Holly said. 'D'you mind if I get my things?'

'Feel free.' The woman moved a few inches along the bed. 'These your sheets are they? Pretty . . .'

'I'll leave them. Use them if you like. I only put them on yesterday.'

'Oh, ta. We're a bit short on sheets. Mickey, that's my three-year-old, he's got what you might call a little problem. Wets the bed sometimes. But your ma said I can use her washer. Nice up here, i'n't it? I hear you're moving down below for a bit.'

'That's right.'

Holly moved silently about the room, wanting to kick the quacking television to pieces and hurl it out of the window. She wouldn't be coming back to this room, so she had to make certain she didn't forget anything. Warm sweaters, jeans, underwear, her toilet things . . . On top of everything, neatly folded into James's rucksack, she placed the rainbow shoes and Little Bear. Then she went downstairs and peeped into the suitcase room. The cases and boxes had been moved to one end and the folding bed put up for her, the saggy old one that they always used when someone stayed the night and there was a Full House.

The window in the suitcase room was high up, like a lavatory window. A line of poetry came to her from something they'd done at school. 'That little patch of blue that prisoners call the sky.' Being in this room would be no better than a prison cell. There was some black mould in one corner and a nasty smell, which Doris said was mice.

Nevertheless she unrolled Rachel's sleeping-bag and set out her toothbrush, towel and flannel, to show she'd moved in. She even put a book on the pillow.

Nobody seemed to be around except the Sinclairs. She could hear voices on the top floor and the smell of cigarettes drifted downwards. Farve would stop that pretty quickly. There might be a good row about it. But she was going to miss it. She wouldn't be here.

She went down the road to the phone-box and rang Jake. When he answered she said, 'So you're still around then.'

'Yep. I'm not going yet. Not till it's quiet. I might go tomorrow morning. Not sure yet. Changed your mind about coming with me then?'

She took a deep breath. 'Yes, I have. Those Sinclair people have been put in my room, while I was out at the Guide meeting. They've just taken over. My stuff's gone to the boxroom. Tell me what I need to bring, but don't say money, because I've not got any.'

'Warm clothes. Food. Toilet-paper. Things you'd need if you were camping.'

'OK. I can get those. When should I meet you? And where?'

There was a pause. 'You can stay the night here if you want. She's gone to London.' He laughed. 'I told her I'd ring the NSPCC. I've got a black eye.'

'You've not.'

'I *have*. Well, I'm getting one.'

On her way home from the phone-box Holly thought rapidly. She had an invitation to go to Rachel's, so she could set off from there for camp. Let them think that's where she'd gone. With luck nobody would check. Muv would be taken up with the Sinclairs and Farve with the festival.

She didn't want to worry Muv. She wanted her to think she was safe at camp, in Clitheroe, and this way she could go with Jake and nobody would be any the wiser.

She would have to make a discreet raid on the spare-food cupboard, a big walk-in closet at the end of the hall which Farve kept locked, because of the drop-ins. It would mean stealing the key.

Taking the food was stealing too, she supposed. But she reasoned it this way: it was payment, really, for all the jobs she did for free.

As she sat in the suitcase room on the sagging camp-bed, she thought again of the muddy, slithery canal towpath, of Jake's slithery eyes when he'd been thieving and of sliding about in general, of not knowing what to hold on to, nor what was *right* to hold on to.

She was sure about certain things, though. Her father and mother were behaving badly to her. In the nicest possible way they were both neglecting her and they needed a shock. And Jake's mother had been both neglectful and cruel.

Finally, she had made a promise to herself that if the Sinclairs moved into her bedroom she would leave home. They had done precisely that and nobody had consulted her. Muv always said that the most important promises were the ones you made to yourself. Well, the time had come for Holly to take her at her word.

Eleven

In her father's study, behind the door, there was an old-fashioned 'key cupboard', where he kept all the household keys on large brass hooks. The cupboard itself was kept locked, but Muv had her own key to it and Holly knew where that was. Muv trusted her. She was often sent to get things out of the store cupboard.

She found her mother's key in an old pottery jar on the larder shelf, unlocked Farve's cupboard with it and made her way to the store cupboard. The coast still appeared to be clear, though she could hear Fat Nan's radio, and upstairs the Sinclairs sounded as if they were having a row.

She opened the cupboard door, switched on the light, and slipped inside. It was an old game cupboard, with hooks for hanging rabbits and hares and pheasants. Now, though, it was filled with the results of Farve's mega monthly shop at the huge Tesco's on the other side of town. There were neat pyramids of tins, and carefully stacked packets, and bumper bags of toilet-rolls. Everything was labelled 'bargain buy' or 'special offer'. Farve always went round the supermarket with his calculator.

If anybody found her, she would have to say that the food was for camp. In any case she couldn't take much. It would have to fit into her rucksack. So she took some toilet-rolls and a few little tins of sausages with beans, a carton of long-life milk and a packet of biscuits. Then she added some tins of tuna-fish and a packet of instant potato. That was all, not much in return for what felt to her like a lifetime of shoe-cleaning, tidying and baby-minding.

In the kitchen she found Muv's second-best can-opener, the blunt one you always had to fiddle with. Nobody would miss that. She also took a couple of carrier-bags, for her washing. Just how she was going to wash her clothes she wasn't quite sure, but she always took a plastic bag for the purpose when she went on holiday. This wasn't a holiday though, it was Running Away.

She packed everything at the bottom of the rucksack, fastened it up and put it on the floor of the Prison Cell. Then she looked at it. This bulging rucksack meant she really was *going*. What must her strategy be now, though? How could she stop them from coming after her?

She would lie low for the rest of the day, pretend to be busying herself in the new room and not get into any arguments about the arrival of the Sinclairs. She would tell Muv, but not Farve, that she'd probably spend the night at Rachel's. 'Probably' somehow made it feel less of a lie. Rachel's father was a doctor and their home number was not in the phone book. That was good. It meant nobody could go checking up on her. She'd go round to Rachel's before bedtime and tell her she wasn't coming to camp. She had a bit of a runny nose and she'd say it was flu. Two other people weren't going already because of flu and Mrs Beresford hadn't seemed bothered. 'More room in the tents,' she'd boomed cheerfully. On second thoughts, perhaps she could just ring Rachel, then Rachel could pass on the message. So that covered everything.

Muv was very, very nice to her, because she'd not made a fuss about the Sinclairs. She said she could go to Rachel's and that Farve wouldn't mind. He was at a rehearsal anyhow, for the festival, and wouldn't be back till late that night. Muv was busy, going from N.O.P. to Fat Nan to the Sinclairs, then back again. There was no time for chatting and so no time for any awkward questions.

At eight o'clock Holly put on the windcheater she'd borrowed from Rachel, shouldered her rucksack and set off for Jake's. She didn't say goodbye to anybody. If she kissed her mother or N.O.P. she knew that she just wouldn't *go*. But it wasn't really official Running Away was it? That meant huge newspaper headlines and tearful appeals on TV. She really didn't want to worry her parents, though a bit of her wanted them to know, one day, that they'd driven her out of her own home by being too taken up with all the needy people, by Farve not listening to her, by Muv being a doormat.

She suspected that Jake *did* want fuss, that he wanted his mother to worry herself sick. 'Are you leaving a note?' she said, as she put her rucksack on the white hall carpet. She could see the coffee 'n tea-leaves stain. It was awful.

'Nope. What would it say if I did? "Have run away"? She'd probably say, "Good riddance." I hope *you've* not left a note. We don't want them coming after us.'

'No. They think I've gone camping. I rang Rachel on my way to you, from a phonebox. Didn't want anyone to hear. I told her to say I'd got flu. Loads of people have. So my parents will just think I've gone away for the weekend.'

'S'pose you have. But it's not just a weekend, you know. I'm serious.'

'How long will we stay?'

'For as long as it takes.'

'Takes to do what?'

'For them all to come to their senses. We don't have to stay at the barn if we don't want to, anyhow. We can move on. We can go to Scotland, or abroad.'

'I've not got a passport,' Holly said. She didn't believe in these plans.

'That's OK. We'll start with Yorkshire. You don't need a passport for that.'

Holly felt secretly relieved. Jake didn't quite believe in his plans either. Well, not the Abroad bit.

He was counting money, loads of it, ten-pound notes and twenty-pound notes, quite a thick wad, when he'd gathered it all together.

'Where did that come from?'

'It's mine. It's what she owes me. My father sends cheques and I'm supposed to have some of the money, but I never get it.'

'You've got lovely things though, Jake,' Holly said, thinking about her little bare attic.

He wrapped the money in a polythene freezer-bag and tucked it into a pouch on the side of his rucksack. Just how he'd come by all those banknotes she thought she would never know. Jake was a mystery.

'We ought to go to sleep early,' he said. 'We're

going on the train. We've got to be at the station by half-past six.'

'*Train*?' That didn't sound like Running Away.

'Well, we can't walk it — though there'll be a big walk at the other end. And we're not hitching lifts. Someone'll spot us.'

'They'll spot us on the train though, won't they?'

'Listen. The train's best. Nobody'll miss us for a day or so, anyhow. Laura's not coming back from London till Monday and you're supposed to be at Guide camp. Got any food?'

She showed him. 'It's not much,' he said.

'Well, it's all I could carry,' she said hotly. 'You don't realize what big trouble I'd be in if my father found out. Nobody's supposed to go into the store cupboard. He'd say it was stealing.'

She wanted to take the word back, but it was too late. Silently Jake turned his face away. He had stolen so many things. What were a few toilet-rolls and some tins of food to him? But to Holly it was big, and so was the tissue of lies she had had to spin to get here at all. She didn't lie very often, but once, when Farve had caught her out, he had quoted some poetry at her:

'Oh what a tangled web we weave
When first we practise to deceive!'

He always hid behind other people, including poets. But it was true — if you practised one untruth, it led to another. And she suspected that the habit was catching, that the whole thing just got bigger and bigger. Certainly she felt thoroughly tangled now.

Jake had gone into his *en suite* bathroom, made some splashing noises and now came back in a dark red towelling bathrobe. 'I'd have a good wash if I were you. I'm not sure when we'll next be able to have one.'

'Isn't there a stream?'

'Yes. It goes past the door.'

'We can use that then.' And they could wash their clothes on flat stones and hang them up to dry on spiky bushes. They could pick berries and eat them. Holly had read about that kind of thing in stories. 'Where can I sleep?' she said. 'I mean tonight?'

Jake looked a bit vague. 'Dunno. Hadn't thought. Hang on, I'll go and investigate.'

In a few seconds he was back. 'You'll have to sleep in my mother's room. There are no sheets on the spare bed. Anyhow, she's got a heater.' Although it was late July, the weather was cold.

'Will it be cold in Yorkshire?' she said, following him into the large front bedroom.

'Colder than here. You did bring warm things, didn't you?'

'I brought what I'd got. Not everyone has

padded ski jackets you know.' For all Jake moaned about his mother it always seemed to Holly that he had piles of the most expensive things. Surely she had bought some of them for him. They couldn't *all* be stolen.

The bedroom was amazing. Holly's mouth dropped open as she stared at the magnificent king-sized bed with its white and gold tasselled counterpane, its heaped up frilly cushions, white alternating with palest lemon, its dove-grey carpet, a luxurious swamp like the carpet on the stairs, its discreet white hanging cupboards with their thin gold beading. By the bed was a small antique chest covered with silver photograph frames. She glanced at them. They all seemed to be of Jake, Jake as a babe-in-arms, Jake toddling, Jake on his first day at primary school, Jake in his St Wilfred's uniform, even the new Jake with a holey sweater whose sleeves came right down over his fingertips, Jake with a complexion like Spotted Dick.

She said, 'I couldn't sleep in here, Jake.'

'You could. She'll never know. Listen, it's a bed isn't it? All you need is to get into bed and go to sleep. You can use my bathroom. I think she'd spot it if someone else had been using hers.'

Gingerly, Holly sat on the bed. It was soft. In her attic the bed was hard. Farve said a firm mattress was better for your back, but she loved beds like this. It seemed to be whispering to her, 'Come on, get in, snuggle down.'

'OK,' she said. 'I'll just have a wash.'

'I'm going to sleep. I'll wake you up at half-past five. G'night, then.'

When she came out of his bathroom − a pigsty like his bedroom − he was already a mere mound under his duvet and was making little snoring noises. Holly crept past. Snoring got on her nerves. How would it be in a barn with nowhere to escape to? And how would she survive in the kind of mess he made? She was going to make it crystal clear from the beginning that there was to be NO MESS. But look at his rucksack, everything stuffed in anyhow, nothing folded up. The only thing he'd taken any care with was the banknotes.

It took her ages to get to sleep. There was so much room in the enormous bed and it was so soft and warm and comforting. She wanted to stay awake, just to enjoy it. It smelled nice, too. The whole room smelled nice. Mrs Tolland had rows and rows of beautiful bottles of stuff, and baskets of soap. Muv never had things like that. When Holly got back she was going to buy her a huge bottle of really expensive perfume. She'd get the money from somewhere.

Thinking about Muv made her feel sad, and a bit scared. She wasn't at Rachel's, all ready for Guide camp. She was an intruder in Jake's mother's bed. What if Mrs Tolland came back, pulled back the covers and found her there? She might yell. She might have one of her Daily Screams, glowering at Holly with those curious glittery eyes and screeching, 'Filth! Vermin! Get out! GET OUT!'

She drifted into an uneasy, light sleep and dreamed of Muv and Farve tramping over the hills, searching, always searching. The dreams were full of close-ups, like a film, of tears rolling down cheeks. The wet face was always Farve's and yet she had never seen him cry, not once, not ever. They were awful dreams.

Dreams were supposed to tell you what was really worrying you and these meant she hated leaving Muv and Farve. But part of her was angry with them too, angry with Farve for the way he treated her, and angry with Muv for letting him. There was a battle going on inside her. Her loyalty to them was having a big fight with her anger.

She didn't sleep much and she was glad when Jake came in with his alarm in his hand. 'Five thirty,' he said. 'Time to get up. But there's no hot water yet. We'll have to use cold.'

Holly shivered as she brushed her teeth. It felt like December, not July. This is how it would be at the barn, but worse, and there'd be no gorgeous bed to sleep in there.

Jake made them porridge for breakfast. She was surprised. She thought he couldn't cook. 'It might be a long day,' he said, writing 'Jake' in syrup on the top of his porridge. 'We've got to stoke up.'

Holly only ate half hers, and none of the toast he'd made. Her insides seemed to be snaking up and down. She felt sick with nerves.

'Let's go, Jake,' she said. He was fiddling with the things on top of his rucksack.

'You're in a hurry all of a sudden.'

'I just want us to go, that's all.'

'Not changed your mind have you?'

'No.'

They walked down the mews a little apart. The houses were silent, all curtains across. They didn't see the twitching of net and the small beady eye peering out of Number 19, where Mr Horne lived.

No, she'd not changed her mind, she said. But that wasn't quite true. This was all part of the tangled web. She was getting more and more enmeshed. It would be simpler to go back to the vicarage with its muddle and its smells. She'd even settle for a few nights in the Prison Cell.

But Jake, having seen the red zigzag station sign, was striding out, chirpy in his wonderful ski jacket. 'Come *on*,' he badgered, 'or we'll miss the train.'

Twelve

Running away was simpler than Holly had imagined, at first anyhow. Jake bought two tickets and gave her one. 'In case we get separated,' he explained. But she did not intend to be separated. Jake was definitely 'in charge' and he'd got all the money.

While he was buying the tickets she looked at a phone-box and wondered whether to phone the vicarage with her green card. Farve insisted on her having that, for emergencies. At least she could tell them, vaguely, that she was about to set off camping. She didn't have to say that she wasn't with Rachel.

But it was as bad as lying, because the idea was to mislead them. There was no difference. Anyhow, the chances were that Farve would still be in bed, not wanting to face the day. And she didn't want to risk talking to her mother. She felt she might cave in, just trickle home to the vicarage. And that would be pathetic. She was *angry* with them, and the last straw had been moving that awful Sinclair family into her bedroom.

She put her green card back into her pocket and moved away from the phone-box, noticing that someone had dumped a stack of local evening papers just outside it, papers left over from the night before. Down the right hand side of the front page was a blank white stripe headed 'Late Newsflashes' and in the middle of this, all smudged, it said 'CHURCH THEFT'. Holly edged sideways and read it. 'A pre-Reformation paten, said to be worth many thousands of pounds, has been stolen from the vicarage of St Bartholomew, Museum Road, Darnley. The paten, usually in the safekeeping of the bank, had been removed to the vicarage for use in the church's forthcoming Patronal Festival when it celebrates a 400-year anniversary. Just how the paten disappeared from the safe, acquired specially for the occasion, remains a mystery.'

Standing squarely in front of the pile of papers Holly felt behind her, ripped off one of the front pages and stuffed it in her pocket. Then she walked up to Jake who was replacing his bank notes in the plastic freezer-bag. Surely he could have nothing to do with the missing gold plate? For one thing it had been locked in a safe and he'd have had to know the combination number in order to open it.

For another he'd have had to know someone who would give him money for it, someone who dealt in ancient silver and gold. The likelihood of Jake's passing the paten to someone in the Manchester underworld was not high. He couldn't have had time, anyway. She'd seen the thing in its jiffy bag less than twenty-four hours ago.

She didn't say anything on the train. It was quite crowded and they couldn't sit together. Jake said that was probably a good thing, that if by any chance someone had worked out they'd run away together and was looking for them they'd attract immediate attention as a pair. He was soon absorbed in the music coming out of his Walkman. The continual tinny buzzing noise reminded her of mosquitoes. She hadn't got one, and the book she'd brought was at the bottom of her rucksack. She stared out of the window, trying not to think about Muv and Farve.

She felt guilty about what she was doing, but at the moment her anger was stronger than her guilt. Since last night at Jake's, two pictures kept creeping into her mind: Mrs Tolland's marvellous bedroom and her own dingy attic at home – *her place*, which they had simply filled up with one of their problem families, without so much as a by-your-leave. It was so awful of them. Well, she wasn't surprised at Farve, he'd done things like that before. But Muv, how could Muv *let* him? Why hadn't she stuck up for Holly?

The landscape moved past, slowly at first as the train trundled through grimy suburbs, past factories and mills, past empty brick-filled patches of waste ground, where fires burned mysteriously and where hunched-up figures shambled about poking paper into the flames with sticks. Gradually the town gave way to country, small flattish fields fuzzed at the edges with thick summer hedges and pierced by the odd church spire. Then, as they moved north, the hills became bigger, swelling up and down more. Holly felt an excitement growing somewhere deep inside her and stared expectantly out of the window. But now the train was really travelling, everything was a greeny-brown flash. A few seats down, his Walkman still glued to him, Jake had fallen asleep with his mouth open. She felt drowsy too. Perhaps she should close her eyes.

But the ticket man was coming down the train. At first she mistook the dark uniform for that of a policeman and her insides flipped right over. What if they'd found out about the stolen gold plate? Or that two kids had run away from Darnley? Disappearing children were 'no big deal' according to Jake, who often talked like film actors on TV. But if one of the children had stolen a valuable antique plate . . .

109

She held out her ticket between two trembling fingers. 'Thanks, love,' the man said, snipping it neatly, and moved down the train. Jake had to be prodded awake by a man in overalls who was sitting next to him. As soon as he'd had his ticket clipped he went to sleep again, only staying awake long enough to put a new tape in his Walkman.

Holly slept too, for a bit. She was hungry, after eating so little of the porridge, and she had no money to buy anything. In her dreams she could smell the hamburgers, toasted sandwiches and coffee that people kept carrying past from the buffet car. After a while there was a big jolt. She opened her eyes and stared out of the window. The sun was shining, and people were looking out on all sides, admiring the landscape. They had stopped in the middle of nowhere.

And it was a marvellous nowhere. The train seemed to have hand-picked its place to stop, just for Holly. The hills, which had grown enormous as she slept, now swept right down to the railway line on each side. They were a marvellous colour, a pale, lemony green, and it looked as if the grass on the lower slopes had just been cut. Far away, in a tiny field, a red tractor was moving slowly up and down and little coloured blobs were following it. Perhaps the farmer was haymaking; she'd read about that in *The Children of Willow Farm*. It was her favourite book, after *Malory Towers*.

There were sheep everywhere, some quite close to the train. They were handsome creatures, with sooty black faces and wonderfully wreathed horns. They looked quite intelligent too, and not at all miserable, not like Doris. Best of all, though, was the stream, sparkling as it rushed down between two hills, emptying itself into a large pool then scampering on again, at the other side, under an old stone bridge. A child in a red T-shirt stood right in the middle, gazing down into the water. Holly stared and stared. She wanted to be that child, and she wanted to open the train windows and hear the water rushing past, see the sheep, and the birds that wheeled above them in the dazzling sky.

Someone prodded her in the back. It was Jake, disentangling himself from his Walkman. 'Got your things?' he said 'We're nearly there. It'll be our station soon.'

'Is it like this, Jake? Is it like this, where we're going?' Holly whispered, turning away from the window reluctantly as the train jolted forwards again. She was in a dream. She wanted to run with the sheep, eat the grass. St Bartholomew's vicarage, the grime of the town, even Muv and Farve had quite faded. There was only This.

111

Jake merely glanced. 'Better,' he said. 'Miles better. Come on, we're stopping.'

Thirteen

It was a very little station and nobody else got off. On both platforms there were big tubs of flowers and a tortoiseshell cat lay curled up on a green bench. A man was sweeping dust up into a plastic bag and everything looked very tidy. It was the kind of station Jake's mother would have approved of.

Holly approved of it too. The snoozing cat and the geraniums gave her a sense of well-being, and she loved the space and silence all around, the hump of green hill over which the track curled like a thin black ribbon. The train was mounting it now, getting smaller and fainter till it became a toy train, then nothing but a blue smudge.

In the ticket-office a man was bent over a type-writer. He was not looking their way, but Jake still pushed her past the glass rather anxiously, glancing this way and that. 'Good thing, these open stations,' he muttered, 'not having a barrier you have to go through. Come on.'

Out in the road he paused and stared round. 'Got to get my bearings,' he said. 'Used to come here with my mother, when they were doing the barn up. Dad used to pick us up and we'd get chips on the way back. They did black peas too. They were fabulous.'

He looked so lost and sad when he spoke that Holly rather wanted to put her arms round him. Instead she said, 'My nan used to make black peas. Perhaps we could get some chips, on our way to the barn.' She was famished.

Jake produced a flat, meaningless smile and tugged his rucksack straight across his shoulders. 'No point in doing that. They'd be cold before we got there and we've got to make a start. It's a long walk.'

'How long?' Holly was wearing her rainbow shoes. The soles were quite thin. Jake had said wear boots, but she hadn't got any.

'Oh, quite a trek.'

'But *how* long?'

Jake was wearing his shifty face. 'I don't know, exactly. About five miles, something like that.'

Holly suspected it was much longer, but Jake obviously wasn't going to tell her. Well, she could manage five miles. She'd done that with Guides. She was hungry though. Back in the station there was a kiosk that sold sweets. 'Could we get some chocolate or something?' she said. 'For the walk?.'

'No. They might notice us.'

'What do you mean, "notice"?'

Jake got exasperated. 'Look,' he said, 'we're on the run. We've gone missing. D'you want them to come and take us back before we've even started?'

'No. No, I don't,' she said. And she didn't, not at that moment. They had run away from their families, to teach them a lesson. No point in caving in before the adventure had even started.

He said, 'I've brought some chocolate, but let's get going. I don't like the look of the weather.'

She stared up as they stepped out. The sky was still bright and the sun still shining, but what had been blue now had a faint yellowish tinge to it and there were one or two big dark clouds, patterning the hillsides with ragged shapes as they floated overhead. 'I'd put your anorak on,' Jake said, pulling his own over his head. 'It'll be pouring down soon.'

When they'd walked a bit he gave her some chocolate; not much, considering the great bag she'd seen in his room. It set her wondering about all his thieving, and about the gold plate that had disappeared from Farve's study. She'd have to ask him about it; she'd got to find out somehow. But she knew she couldn't plunge straight in. That always drove him into a corner, gave him his frightened-rabbit look, when she was sure he automatically told lies. So she walked at his side in silence, hearing nothing but her own laboured breathing as the road got steeper, and the peevish little wind that had got up, rattling away in the hedges. There was a mutter of distant thunder and no sun, now.

Whenever he heard the noise of a car engine Jake made her walk a few yards in front of him. He said they mustn't look like a couple who were doing things together. Once, when there was a gateway, he ran into a field and crouched behind the hedge until the car had gone past. It frightened Holly. They had run away to throw off all the rules and regulations of home, but they weren't really free. It felt to her as if they were both frightened. Deep down she was a bit frightened of him too. He was so moody and tense. He clearly wasn't enjoying running away much.

After they'd done a couple of miles she asked him when they might get their first sight of the barn. 'Not for ages,' he said, plodding on. He was slower than she was; he didn't get much exercise, sitting in his room so much, watching videos. 'And don't start that,' he added irritably.

Anger stirred in her. There was no need to say that. She wasn't 'starting' anything. How did she know where his precious barn was? All she could see were the endless green hills, browsing sheep, streams, the odd glint of falling water, and, over everything, the great sky. Yes, it was beautiful, just as he'd promised. They could have a great time in a place like this. But he'd brought in a sour note now, being so critical of her. She went for him.

'I saw a paper on the station in Darnley,' she said. 'There was a newsflash. Someone's pinched that gold plate my father took out of the bank. Was it you?'

She stared hard at him, trying to judge his reaction, thinking she saw, just for a split second, a flicker of genuine surprise. He said nothing for a minute, then he screwed his mouth up into a tiny crooked line. 'Perhaps it was.'

She grabbed his arm and forced him to slow down. 'What do you mean, "perhaps"? Did you or didn't you?' She wasn't really confident that someone as disorganized as Jake was capable of pulling off a serious thing like stealing the plate, but if he *had* done, then it was outrageous. And how could he have done it to Farve when Holly was supposed to be his best friend?

They stood in the middle of the road together, Holly glaring at him and waiting for an answer, her nails digging into his arm, Jake sullen, hanging his head.

Suddenly a lorry came round the corner and screeched to a halt. They jumped out of the way as the driver unwound his window, waiting for him to swear at them. But he actually offered to give them a lift. 'No thanks,' Jake said politely, 'we're doing a project. We can't accept lifts. People are sponsoring us for charity.'

'OK, pal, good on yer.' The cheery-faced man at the wheel waved and drove off. Holly was amazed at the ease of Jake's lying. It would never have occurred to her to say anything like that. But she had not forgotten the gold plate. She *would* get the truth out of him.

He decided they must get off the road. He said there were too many cars going past and that sooner or later someone was going to ask questions. So they pushed through a tangled, thorny hedge, crossed a couple of wide fields and set off along a thin, stony track that seemed to lead right into the middle of the endless hills. Holly could feel every pebble through the soles of her rainbow shoes. She'd got blisters on both heels and it was raining hard. She wanted to go to the loo. It was all right for boys. Jake had just turned his back on her, when he wanted to go. Girls couldn't do that. Would there be a loo at the barn? Had his parents put one in before they'd abandoned the project? And what if someone else was using it? It was July, after all – holiday time. Had Jake actually thought of that?

Suddenly she felt really angry with him. She gambled. She said, 'You did take the plate, didn't you?'

He smirked slightly. 'We needed the money to do this you know, and my mother's bank card's been stopped. She must have found out.'

'You mean you knew the number, for her hole-in-the-wall card?'

'Let's say I made it my business to get the number.'

He was talking big, but somehow she felt sorry for him, trying to behave like some smart TV crook. 'Listen,' he said feverishly, suddenly Jake again, 'I've told you, she owes me *loads* of money. My dad sends cheques and I never get anything.'

'But she buys you things,' Holly pointed out. 'You get nice clothes.'

'Cash in hand, that's what she's supposed to give me. I had a right to that money. Anyhow, it's over now. She's twigged. She must have put a stop on her bank account.'

'But, I mean, didn't you *talk* about it? Didn't she want to know what you were playing at?'

'We never talk,' he said bitterly.

They walked on. 'So you did a deal with some-one over the plate?'

119

'What if I did?' he grunted. 'Thought it was rather good, getting my hands on that.'

For a few seconds she was speechless. 'Rather good,' she stammered at last, *rather good*! Didn't you stop to think how it might affect *me*? I mean, it does involve my father.'

'Thought you didn't like your father. Thought you were sick of him. Thought you'd be pleased, me getting the money for this trip and everything. You're just ungrateful, that's what you are. Where would you be, without me?'

He turned his face away from her and she saw that he was trying very hard not to cry. She had seen him like this before, when he talked about the way his parents treated him. It was daft, this idea that boys weren't allowed to cry. That was one of the things wrong with Farve, the way he squashed his feelings all the time. She felt sorry for Jake, but somehow she didn't quite trust him. He was twisting things.

She said, 'I'm not ungrateful, really I'm not. Only, you can't blame me for getting angry when you've robbed my father.' But she was twisting things herself now. His dishonesty must be catching. She really still couldn't believe that he'd stolen the plate.

For a start, if he had, how on earth had he opened the study safe? He must, somehow, have known the combination on the lock. Someone had chucked the old safe out and that's how Farve had come to have it. She said, 'How did you —' But then she broke off abruptly. He had stopped in his tracks and turned very pale.

'What's the matter?'

'I don't get this.'

'Get what?'

'Well, from here you should be able to see . . . perhaps I'm in the wrong field.'

'The barn?' she said eagerly. 'You mean we can see the barn from here? Well, we've found the stream. Let's follow it.'

'OK. The barn's down at the bottom.' But his voice was weirdly flat, and now he was following her, having been the leader since they'd left Darnley-in-Makerfield.

Pushing through tall wet bracken that slapped her sodden legs, slipping on muddy stones at the edge of the tumbling water, she came at last to a clump of little trees, and a gate to the left of them.

'Where now?'

'Through the gate, but I've told you, I just don't get it.'

She pushed open rusty red bars and stood in a broad sloping field. The stream, also broader now, rushed away down the hill. The rain had stopped and a bird was twittering somewhere as the sun

121

came out grudgingly for a minute from under the thick cloud.

'It was here,' Jake said blankly, and his hand was trembling as he pointed at the grass. 'Here, where this wall is. But someone's pulled it down. It's gone.'

Fourteen

Holly stared at him in alarm, then grabbed him, because he seemed to be swaying about. 'I think you'd better sit down,' she said, and they both sat down on the sodden grass. For a minute he had difficulty getting his words out. Then he said, in a kind of whisper, 'I feel as if someone's kicked me in the stomach. I can't get my breath.'

Holly knew that feeling. She'd had it the day they pulled down the little primary school at the end of Museum Road, the school where she'd been so happy. It was such a funny little place, with a pointed tower and a bell and faded squares for hopscotch painted on the playground. She'd loved it. Then, one morning, she'd seen a horrible machine in front of it, unloading chains and a great iron ball to smash the walls down. Next day there was nothing there at all, except rubble and dust. It was as if all her happy memories had been swallowed up into a kind of swirling emptiness. Jake must be

123

feeling it now, the same awful hollowness.

He said, 'The people who bought it must've gone bust, or something. They must've sold it to someone for the stone and things. Stone's worth quite a bit.'

'Perhaps they couldn't get permission to make it into a real house,' Holly suggested. 'Farve had to apply for permission to build the church loos, and they made a fuss, because the building was in a book or something.'

'I don't know . . .' Jake's voice was defeated. 'I don't think my father asked anyone's permission. Anyhow, what's the point of talking about it now? They've pulled it down.'

It was raining again. Holly felt very cold and ravenously hungry. NO BARN. So was this the end of the adventure? Were they simply going to walk back to the little station and get a train back to Darnley? How pathetic. There must be *somewhere* else they could go, surely? Jake had stood up and was looking up and down the field. 'There are lots of these barns,' he said. 'There was one at the bottom of the next field. I used to play in it. S'pose they've pulled that down as well.' He still looked defeated, very crumpled and small.

'Well, we can always see,' Holly said. They had to shelter somewhere. She slung on her rucksack and started walking down the meadow. 'Pooh,' she said, wrinkling her nose. 'What on earth's that?' It was a sweet, sickly, sewery smell and it was doing nasty things to her yawning insides.

'Dunno,' Jake said miserably, pushing on. When they'd scrambled over the broad stone wall at the bottom of the field they found out. There was a small, neat barn, just as Jake had said, the one he used to play in. But the field that dropped away from it contained not the usual black-faced sheep, but several large pigs. Dotted over the grass were little tin houses for them, a bit like baby air-raid shelters.

Jake sniffed. 'You're right, they do stink. They didn't used to be here. This is all sheep country.'

Holly felt quite pleased to see them. She'd always been fond of pigs and they were supposed to be intelligent creatures. Muv had a mad theory about them. She said they might be the Missing Link, the bit that fitted in between Monkey and Man. Holly stared at them, peacefully rooting about among the tussocks of grass. Poor Fat Nan had been a bit like a prize porker, stuck to the bath-mat. Ought she to go home? Ought she to go home *now*? What if they'd discovered that she'd tricked them? She felt a pang of homesickness, but she crushed it. It was Muv and Farve who'd tricked *her*, installing that family in her attic. They needed to learn a lesson. Anyhow, she and Jake had got this far without being caught and they were going to make the best of it, even if there was no barn.

He was untying some pink twine that fastened a door to an iron hasp. 'They keep their rams in here sometimes,' he said, 'But it's empty.' Holly peered in, over his shoulder. The barn was filled with straw and there was a dustbin in one corner. Jake went in, lifted the lid and sniffed. 'It's for the pigs, I suppose. It's pellets. Come on, let's see what upstairs is like. It used to be a good place to play. I used to make dens in it.'

Holly didn't think barns had an 'upstairs', but then she saw narrow stone steps slotted into a side wall, and at the top another double door tied up with twine. She followed Jake up and inside and saw that this part was empty. It even had a wooden floor. 'What would this be for then?' she said.

'Storing things – and I suppose they used to sleep here too, in the summer. The farm's miles away.'

In the wall opposite the door there was a tiny window. Holly went across to it and looked out. What she saw took her breath away, but it wasn't that awful stomach-squeezing feeling she'd had when they'd pulled the school down, it was the breathlessness of sheer wonder.

She could see hills – 'fells' Jake sometimes called them – one folded upon another in a marvellous pattern of gentle curves. Sheep speckled the green grass, and higher, nearer the skyline, was a wide dark band of bracken – or was it heather? Both grew here, she had seen them from the road as they'd done their long trek. Bigger, greyer dots were little barns, like this one, and the flatter fields were turned into patchwork by ancient stone walls. The view all seemed to spring from a river that had carved its way down through the hills, a dark blue river with thickly wooded banks, trees of all kinds of green. She had never seen so many greens. But what was best wasn't what she saw but what she heard. Absolutely nothing, so that the nearby chomping of the pigs felt loud. The land itself was most wonderfully silent. She and Jake might have been the only people on earth.

He said, 'It's not bad, is it?'

Holly turned away from the window. The view was marvellous, but the barn itself ... it wasn't exactly what she had imagined. She said, 'Do you mean to stay in, to sleep in, and everything?'

'Well, we could. It's dry. We could put some of that straw down here, and make our beds on that, you know, with our sleeping bags. It'd be a bit softer.'

'But there's no – how do we wash?'

'There's that stream. It's not exactly running past the door, but it is *there*.'

'There's no loo,' said Holly. She'd expected a real house, a house made from a barn, but a house nevertheless.

'We don't need a loo. We can go — anywhere.'

'S'pose we'll have to.' But she was thinking they would have to go in different directions. And the pigs were to be avoided on such expeditions. Unlike Jake she was quite particular in her personal habits. She now realized that she should have thought more about the loo arrangements.

Jake seemed to have cheered up and he'd started to unpack his rucksack. 'Got any sellotape?'

'*Sellotape?* Are you joking?'

'No. I just thought we ought to stick something over this window. It'll get cold tonight.'

'Could we use sticking-plasters? I've got a couple of those.'

'I'll have a go. Want something to eat?'

'Yes please.'

He gave her a Crunchie bar, but somehow she didn't feel like it. She wanted something that felt like an official meal, some meat and potatoes, something hot. There was nothing to drink unless one of them went to the stream and that was three steep fields away.

Jake had unrolled his sleeping-bag and was fiddling with a bright blue canister.

'What's that?'

'A camping stove. Thought I might heat something up. I've got some beans.'

'And I've got a tin-opener.'

But they had no plates and no spoons and the stove kept going out. They had to eat the beans out of the tiny saucepan Jake had brought, sharing the knife on his 'desk organizer' to scoop them up. Before they'd finished eating them they were stone-cold. Holly made an expedition to the stream with a plastic bottle and filled it with water. Jake had brought tea-bags, but before they could boil the water they had to clean the pan out. That meant another trek to the stream. The tea was lukewarm, like the beans, and tasted of tomato sauce. Holly couldn't drink it. She felt a bit sick. Unrolling her sleeping-bag she lay down in a corner, using her lumpy rucksack as a pillow.

Almost immediately something ran over her hand and scuttled into a corner. She shrieked and leapt up. 'What on earth was that?'

Jake, who'd been staring out of the window, leapt towards her and clapped his hand over her mouth. 'Shuddup, you silly cow. There's somebody out there, seeing to the pigs. D'you want them to hear you? Now, SHUDDUP!'

F i f t e e n

With his hand still rammed up against her mouth he shunted them both over to the window and pointed down silently. A boy was standing in the field just below them, staring at the barn. He was older than they were — eighteen, perhaps — and fat, with swollen pink cheeks that seemed to push his eyes up into his forehead and shrink them. He had a flat, squashed-up face and a very wide nose that was so tip-tilted the nostrils were like two big holes. If he was looking after the pigs it was a perfect job for him, thought Holly, because, really, he looked like a pig. In pigs the bulgy cheeks and wide snout were all right. They didn't look good on humans though. They looked ugly, and this boy was ugly. She wouldn't have minded if he'd had a kind expression. You couldn't help how you looked, after all. But his face wasn't kind. It was suspicious and greedy. She very much wanted him to go away.

He didn't, not for ages. He just went on staring at the barn. Then he bent down and seemed to be inspecting the grass very carefully. It was all flat under the window where they'd sat looking at the amazing view. Jake had smoked and they'd eaten some chocolate. The pig boy had probably found the wrappers. Jake was rather dirty in his personal habits, she'd noticed. He never put anything in litter-bins. Farve was crazy about that. He'd smacked her and James for dropping litter, when they were little. She was trying to keep the barn clean and tidy. After all, it was their home, for now anyway. But he was no different in the barn from the way he was at home. His end of it was already a tip.

At last they thought the boy was going away and Jake relaxed his grip on her, then the boy seemed to change his mind and they heard him push open the door of the barn underneath them. Holly started to panic. It was very dusty in the upstairs room. What if one of them sneezed? What if one of them lost their balance and fell, making the floorboards creak? He'd be up after them, and her bones told her he might turn nasty.

They heard shuffling noises and humming, then the clash of the dustbin lid. Through the little window they watched him go into the field and scatter something on the grass, some kind of food from the bin, presumably. The pigs lumbered up grunting. Eventually they heard the roar of an engine being kicked into life and revved up, and they saw the pig boy shoot away down the field on a motorbike, riding the bumps with skill. The pigs took no notice of the din. They just went on munching.

'Phew!' Jake relaxed his hold on her, slumped down on to his sleeping-bag and lit a cigarette. 'That was a near thing.' Holly sat down too. The smoking was starting to get on her nerves. This space was too confined for it and it made her cough. She said, 'I think you ought to smoke outside. It makes it too stuffy up here. Anyhow, it's dangerous, with the straw and everything.'

Jake smoked on. This was his pattern if she mentioned something she didn't like, just to pretend she'd not spoken. 'S'pose he'll be back in the morning,' he said. 'We'd better work out his times for doing things and make sure we're not around. What time is it?'

'I don't know. I forgot my watch.'

He pulled a face. 'So did I. So we won't know what time it is, will we?' He looked furious. As if it was her fault.

She shrugged. 'Well, it's getting dark. I'm going to sleep.'

'Don't you want anything else to eat?'

'No. I don't fancy anything.' She did. She fancied

crisp bacon and fat sausages, crunchy fried bread and mushrooms and about a gallon of hot tea. Cold beans out of a tin weren't the same.

'Can I borrow the torch?' she said, once she was inside her sleeping-bag. She always liked to read before she went to sleep and she'd brought her favourite *Malory Towers* book.

There was silence, then a piggy little grunt.

'Forgot it, didn't I?'

'Oh *no*!' This meant hours and hours in the dark, with no way of knowing where you were. She thought again of the Thing that had scurried over her hand and her insides shrivelled.

'Well, *you* could have brought one.'

'I told you, I've not *got* a torch.'

'Well, neither have I now, so that makes two of us.'

'Oh, drop dead,' she wanted to say, but instead she stuck her thumb in her mouth and sucked it. When desperate it was the one way she could get to sleep.

It was a horrible night. The stuffy upper room smelt of Jake's cigarettes and of pigs and sweat. Once she had to get up to do a wee, in the pitch darkness, stumbling down the slithery stone steps and blindly squatting amongst bushes that prickled her bottom. After that she couldn't get to sleep again. Jake was snoring, and now and again he

133

broke wind. If she added up all the various smells it was nightmarish. No wonder she kept feeling sick. The only good smell was of home. It came from her old blue cardigan, the one she always wore in bed. She buried her nose in it, trying to blot out the unpleasant smells of Jake, and lay there, waiting for the morning to come, watching the square of sky through the little window lighten first to grey, then to pink, then to pale blue. At least the weather looked settled. They could have a great time here, if only she got on a bit better with Jake. But she obviously irritated him, and his unpleasant habits got on her nerves. It was OK camping in a barn with someone you liked, but here they didn't have the comforts and conveniences of home. Here it was life in the raw, a floor to sleep on, cold baked beans to eat and going to the loo in the bushes. It was enough to test any friendship and theirs wasn't doing so well.

She got up while Jake was still asleep, took her towel and toothbrush and soap and went to find somewhere to wash. Getting clean felt more important than eating, after her smelly night. She felt she must now reek, like a bit of bad fish.

After yesterday's rain the stream was full and rushing. She wandered along the bank and eventually settled on a place where there was a wide, shallow waterfall emptying itself into quite a deep pool. She decided to wash her feet and her legs, so she balanced her rainbow shoes on a rock and waded forward.

Ouch! The brownish water was freezing. She wanted to get straight out. If she stayed there she'd surely get frost bite. But she told herself very sternly that she was being pathetic. She let the water swish round her ankles while she rubbed away with the soap and after a bit it didn't seem quite so cold.

She got bolder, splashed her face and gave herself a good wash, then she brushed her teeth. It was only as she lifted her head from spitting the pink peppermint foam away into the whirling stream that she saw her rainbow sneakers floating away in the current. Somehow, and she thought she'd been so careful, they had been placed too near the water. Or perhaps she'd made waves while she was washing. 'Hey!' she shouted, and, hobbling out on to the bank over painful pebbles, she tried to grab at them from the dry land. But she was too late and in any case the water twisted away and was lost in thick greenery. She sat on the bank and cried.

Someone was laughing at her, and pointing, the pig boy with his horrible black nostrils, leaning on his motorbike. 'That's great, that is,' he was saying, and his speech was slurred as if he was drunk.

'Oh yes,' she said, instantly recovering herself. She wasn't going to cry in front of anyone, least of all this pig boy. 'It's marvellous, when your shoes get washed away. You should try it sometime. Bare feet are good for you, especially when there's a lot of pig muck around.' And wrapping her washing things neatly in her towel she began to make her way up the fields towards the barn, carefully avoiding the droppings. The pigs took no notice. They were too busy grubbing away to find what the boy had scattered over the grass.

He started his bike up and followed her. As they reached the barn Jake came out with a cigarette. 'You camping out in there or summat?' His voice was distinctly unfriendly and Holly could feel Jake go all prickly.

'What if we are?' he said in a dangerous voice. 'It's a free country. We're not doing any harm.'

'Where you from then?' The pig boy had folded his arms and was leaning forward on his bike.

'Mind your own business,' Jake said.

'Yes, why don't you?' Holly said supportively. 'Just, just push off.' She hadn't liked it when he'd laughed about her shoes floating away.

But he was staring hard at them, his small squashed-up eyes flicking from one to the other then back again. 'You're them kids, aren't you? It's been on the news about you. You're from Darnley.'

There was a long, awful silence broken only by the chattering of the stream and a bird singing heartlessly in a tree that overhung the barn. It was the most hideous bad luck that this evil-looking boy had heard about them running away. ON THE NEWS. It must mean that both Muv and Farve *and* Mrs Tolland had told the police. People must be searching for them now, this minute. Perhaps Jake *had* stolen Farve's gold plate. That would be why they had become an official news item. A bit of Holly was relieved. The prospect of spending days in the draughty barn with Jake breaking wind and mice running over her was not attractive. But rather more of her was disappointed. After all it *was* an adventure. They *had* run away. They were an official newsflash. What a comedown to be hauled back home by furious parents, when things had only just started.

But perhaps this boy was lying. He spoke in a peculiar, drunken way and he looked odd. Perhaps there was something a bit wrong with his brain. But he couldn't have invented the bit about them coming from Darnley, could he? No. It had to be true. He'd guessed who they were.

Jake suddenly had a personality change. 'Want a fag?' he said. 'I've got loads. By the way, we're from Birmingham, y'know, the Black Countree. I'm called Mick, and this is my cousin Sally.' Holly listened in awed admiration. The accent was perfect.

But the pig boy remained suspicious, hesitated and looked furtively round him. Then he took the cigarette from between Jake's fingers. 'Well, OK then. Ta.' He giggled. 'My ma's gonna kill me though.'

'Hang on a minute,' Jake said, running up the stone steps into the upper room. 'You can have a whole pack.'

He came down with his rucksack, fished in a side pocket and brought out a new pack of cigarettes. 'Here, take them. They won't bite. Go on.' He spoke as if he was talking to a little child. He'd obviously decided that the boy wasn't right in the head.

The pig boy pocketed the cigarettes, then said immediately, 'I'm still telling my ma about you. You bin on the news.'

'Listen, mate,' Jake said, still doing his Birmingham accent, 'We've got nothing to do with any missing kids. We're just camping for the weekend, on our own, you know, like people do. Like those people at the bottom of the hill. That's your campsite isn't it?'

'Yeah. And you have to pay good money to camp there. My dad gets a ton of money from the campers. He doesn't give me none though. He's mean as muck, my dad is.'

Jake dug into his rucksack, turned his back and scrabbled, then advanced on the pig boy with two bank notes. 'Here's some money, and there's more where that came from. Don't tell on us, *please*,' he pleaded.

The pig boy's eyes grew large and, instantly, he pocketed the cash. 'OK then. You can stay. I'll not tell.'

Seconds later he was roaring off down the field in a great burst of sound after which the deep silence felt uncanny. It was as if all the noise in the world had suddenly been switched off. Jake and Holly looked at each other then, sheepishly. Jake inspected the tops of his boots. Holly said quietly, 'That was a very, very stupid thing to do.'

'Why was it? We don't need all the money. I mean, we can't *go* anywhere, specially not now. We've got to keep out of sight. *Why* was it stupid?'

'Because he'll be back, that's why,' she told him. 'Because he'll want more. We ought to go somewhere else. We're trapped.'

Sixteen

Going anywhere else was easier said than done, because Holly had no shoes. Jake went down to the stream to see if they were stuck between the stones, but he came back empty-handed. 'We can have a look further down,' he said, 'but we'll have to be careful. It comes out near the camp-site.'

'And what am I supposed to do till we find them?' Holly said grumpily. She was now thoroughly fed up with Jake, fed up with his endless cigarettes, the way he smelt, even the way he looked. Most irritating of all was his weird ability to shut out reality.

It had been mad, giving the pig boy money, and she had tried very hard to get him to give the rest to her to look after. But he wouldn't. He promised grudgingly to put it in a safe place in the barn, in case the boy came back. But she had a strong feeling that he didn't really have his mind focused on looking after it. She had decided he only lived for the moment.

As soon as the motorbike had roared off across the field he seemed to think they were saved. And she still wondered what they were going to *do*, now they'd got here. The countryside was beautiful, the loveliest landscape she'd ever seen. And the barn was OK, at least in the daylight, with the sun shining. But she had no shoes, and even if she'd not lost them she suspected that Jake wouldn't have wanted to budge from the barn and go on walks. He'd liked the idea of the place but really he was a town person. Look how he listened to his Walkman all the time. She suspected he'd have rigged up a TV if it had been practical. His dad had had a TV in the barn they'd pulled down; they'd watched football on it together. That seemed to be one of his happier memories.

She put on two pairs of thick socks, and on top of them a pair of Jake's hiking socks. Then, together, they made their way down the field and along the stream, looking all the time for the rainbow shoes. In spite of three layers, the ground felt very hard. Her feet were soon sore, and it was difficult keeping close to the stream. It kept diving under low-growing trees or it disappeared under the ground altogether.

At last it flattened out into quite a river, with fairy-tale stepping-stones, all white and gleaming, to get you across to a camp-site on the other side. There were several tents dotted over a broad field, with cars drawn up close to them, and a road beyond the grass. People were moving about, fiddling with camping stoves and hanging out washing on little plastic lines. Quite near the stream three young children were playing tick.

'My shoes, look, they're there!' Holly had spotted them, down below the stepping-stones, stuck in a bend of the river where a tree spread out over the water.

'Shut UP!' Jake hissed in her ear. 'D'you want someone to see us? Keep out of sight. Listen, we'd better go back to the barn. There are too many people about.'

'But what about my *shoes*? It's all right for you. You've got boots on. How would you like to be walking about in your stockinged feet?'

'I'll come back and get them, when it's a bit quieter. Most people'll go off for the day. I'll come and get them then. Let's have some breakfast.'

'I don't want any. I'm sick of cold food.' Holly felt like crying about her shoes. The children playing reminded her of N.O.P. and of holidays with James when they were little. There'd been some good times then, some family times. She missed everyone at home and she knew they must be worried sick about her, even if Jake's mother wasn't worrying. She would be though. She did care about him in her own weird way. Look at all those photos up in the gold and white bedroom.

When they got to the field where the pigs were, Jake told her to stay by the stone wall, and to crouch down, just in case the pig boy was around or, worse, one of his parents. But there was no sign of the motorbike, and the pigs were peacefully rooting round in the grass. They took no notice when Holly and Jake hurried past, up to the barn. Holly picked up one of the pellets they'd been given and put it in her mouth. It tasted of cardboard with sugar sprinkled on it. 'Yuk,' she said, spitting it away.

'What d'you want to go and do that for?' Jake was staring at her as if she was loopy.

'Dunno. Perhaps I'm coming out in sympathy with the pigs. We'll start smelling like them soon. I thought you said there was somewhere to swim. I want a proper wash.'

'There is, a great place, right away from everything. Let's eat something first though.'

While the water was boiling and Jake was outside smoking – he'd agreed to go outside, as long as it wasn't raining – she tried to make it civilized inside the barn, rolling up their sleeping-bags and arranging their rucksacks neatly against the wall, with Little Bear sitting on top of hers. But there was still nothing to put their food on, when it was ready, and there was something horrible about trying to spoon it from a tin into your mouth. She suddenly remembered the 'pig bucket', in which Muv saved things like potato peelings, to spread on the garden and she thought again about that curious pellet she'd eaten. In the Bible the son who ran away ate 'husks'. That was old-fashioned pig food, apparently. When she was little she'd thought it was 'rusks' — baby food, the things N.O.P. threw round.

She found herself thinking of the painting in St Bartholomew's, and of the polished, baby head of the son kneeling at his father's feet. The son's shoes were worn through, just like her socks would be if she didn't get the missing sneakers back soon, and she'd start smelling really bad, just as he must have smelt. The picture, with the kneeling son and the old blind father was somehow all mixed up with the idea of pigswill and having to pee in the bushes and of not having anywhere to sleep at night, not sleep properly anyhow. Without warning, tears welled up in her eyes. Suddenly she wanted to sit down and cry about everything. But she was trying to make some tea that didn't taste of baked beans, so she had to concentrate. When Jake came back, she was still snuffling, her head bent over the little tin saucepan.

He was full of well-being after his smoke in the

sunshine, and he didn't seem to notice. They ate baked beans (again) and tuna-fish, followed by biscuits and tea. At least this time it was hot, more or less. The one advantage of eating out of tins was that you didn't have to do any washing-up, but it did mean you got sticky. Jake couldn't understand why she kept going to wash at the stream. He seemed to quite like being dirty; she wondered if it comforted him in some way. Wherever he was he made a nest of rubbish round himself and just snuggled into the middle of it. He said mess was part of his artistic temperament and that if you got too fussy about being tidy you'd never create anything. '"A tidy house means a bored woman",' he told her, as she tried to wipe dust from the floor with some rolled-up socks. 'I gave my mother a badge with that on.'

'Did she wear it?'

'No. She was mad with me. She threw it away.'

'Well, my mother'd love a tidy house,' Holly said sneezing, as the dust came up in thick brown puffs. 'She's just not got time though. My father's tidy. And I am.'

'Yes. I've noticed,' Jake said rather gloomily, absently fishing for his cigarettes, then, seeing her face, putting them away again.

'It doesn't mean you're bored, you know, or boring,' Holly informed him. 'It just means, well, that you like to know where things are.' In her mind's eye she could see Farve's study with its little pot of sharpened pencils, his paperweight in the shape of a frog, that Muv had given him, and his tiny maroon school cap that hung from the door on a brass hook. Fat Nan had kept that, from when he was a little boy. To her surprise, Holly was missing her father much more than she'd ever expected, missing him as much as Muv and N.O.P.

'Wonder what they're doing?' she said in a miserable voice.

'Who?'

'The old folks at home.'

'Dunno. If she *is* at home, and that'd make a change, my mother'll be doing something like cleaning cupboards out, or shampooing things that don't need it, or rubbing non-existent scratches off the furniture. She's manic.'

'No. She's unhappy, that's all.' Holly understood why Mrs Tolland was mad on order and neatness. It was because she needed to control something. There was so much she couldn't control, like Jake. Holly kept her attic room at the vicarage spick and span because everywhere else was such a mess. But she didn't explain to Jake about the workings of his mother's mind. She thought he might not like it. Instead she said, 'What d'you think mine are doing then?'

Jake gave a little smile. 'They're probably out on the streets, collecting a few tramps. Honestly, I don't know how you stick it. Want to see something I've done?'

He dug into his rucksack and brought out a polythene bag full of papers.'

'What's that?'

'Things for the *Daily Scream.*'

'Oh. Really?' She had forgotten all about it, after they'd started planning to run away.

'I did this,' Jake said, handing her a drawing. 'It's a kind of trap, for when parents go snooping.'

Holly looked at the piece of paper. It was a cartoon and it was of Farve. Yes, it was most definitely Farve, standing in the doorway of Holly's attic with a telescope in one hand and a magnifying glass in the other. At the top it said, 'ARE YOUR PARENTS SNOOPERS?' Then, in smaller print, 'Why not invest in the Tolland-Berry MANTRAP and end snooping for ever?' The 'Mantrap' was a pair of lethal spiked jaws, wide open, just inside the door, ready to close upon any snooping parent tempted by the bait. This consisted of a pile of little people, all labelled. 'Typical Tramp', Holly read. 'Juicy Dropout', 'Four-Person Family, Problems Guaranteed.' Cartoon Farve, impossibly tall and bristly, with great big teeth, was rubbing his hands and slavering in anticipation.

Jake looked pleased. 'D'you like it?' he said.

'Well, ye-es,' she replied rather slowly. 'It's a brilliant cartoon.' But Holly wasn't sure she *did* like it. She rather admired Farve for giving his time to so many pathetic people. It was better than shampooing clean carpets, anyway. She fished in the polythene bag. 'What's this?'

'"The Great Sneaker Mystery". I've only just started that. It's the serial. You know, about when your father hid your shoes.'

'Oh yes,' she said in a small voice. 'I'm not sure . . .'

'Well, it was your idea. You said we could have an episode each week.'

'Yes, I know, but . . .' She didn't much want to now, in spite of what Farve had done. She just wanted to see him. Hiding her shoes didn't feel all that important any more, but running away did. She kept thinking of how worried Farve had been when she'd stayed out late at Jake's, and how much more worried he'd be now she'd gone missing. He'd be out of his mind. So would Muv. Why had she ever let Jake persuade her?

She decided to change the subject.

'I found some things in one of our Oxfam boxes,' she said. 'Things that belonged to my parents. There were a lot of those very wide ties –'

'Kipper ties.'

148

'Yes. Is that what they're called? Well, there were those. And a trouser-suit that Muv wore on her honeymoon, bright purple.'

'Yuk. What else?'

'Some flared jeans, of Farve's. I thought we might have a little feature: 'Antiques Road Show', something like that. It could be quite funny.'

'Good idea. Thought of anything else?'

'Well, what about money? I mean, my parents, they have this *ridiculous* attitude. They will *not* give me any independence. They just say, 'You only have to ask.' Things like that. But I don't *like* asking. And I shouldn't have to.' Holly realized that she was still pretty cross with her parents about a lot of things. She did wish she could talk to them though. She felt sure they'd be much more reasonable now, since the running away.

Jake said, 'It could go in DORIS'S DAILY DIARY. Subtitle: "Going Through a Phrase" ... "You only have to ask." That's one. Oh yes, and "Money Doesn't Grow On Trees".'

'"You don't know you're born",' Holly said miserably. 'I think that's the stupidest one, only ... only ...'

'Only *what?*' Jake said, busy scribbling. He sounded rather irritable.

'Well, if you think about it, there must be a *reason* why parents go on, saying the same boring things day after day. Perhaps it's because they get fed up with us.' She didn't like to admit it, but it had just occurred to her that parents had their point of view as well, that they got depressed with the way things were. It wasn't just one-way traffic. It couldn't be. But she decided not to go into this with Jake. He seemed much too angry with his mother to see reason.

'We could do a Survival Guide,' she said, opting for rather safer territory. 'We could write about trying to survive in this barn, for example. You know, make it like the adventures of Robinson Crusoe.'

'That's good,' Jake said, starting a new piece of paper.

'Going to the loo among the pigs,' she murmured. 'The way spikes stick into your bottom.'

'Mice running over you.'

'Tea that tastes of tomato sauce.' The more she thought about it the less and less it felt like an adventure. 'Come on,' she said, getting to her feet. 'The sun's out. Let's go to the bathing place. You stink.'

It was a long walk and there were a lot of stones. A hole got rubbed through on her left heel and it started to bleed. She was limping as they scrambled up the rocks by the side of the stream.

Jake had been very quiet all the way, but she'd felt an excitement in him. Now he whispered, 'It's OK, we're here. Look at it. Nobody ever comes here you see, too much of a walk. It's brilliant. We can swim here. Look, just look at it.'

He pushed aside thick green branches, wriggling through a gap and she wriggled through after him. Then they both stood upright. What had been a muted, far-off rushing noise was now a crash and a roar. It was a sheet of creamy-brown water hurling itself off a broad, flat rock that spanned the wide stream into a blue-black pool below. Near the waterfall the pool looked broody and deep, but near the edge it barely lapped over the stones.

Jake stripped off, down to some floppy boxer shorts with Noddy and Big Ears on them. Then he waded out towards the middle of the pool and started swimming. The sun was shining on the water and filtering through the trees, making coins of gold light. It looked gorgeous. Jake was doing a steady breast-stroke towards the waterfall. When he got there she saw him push himself up on to a flat rock near the bottom and sit there with the water gushing over him. 'It's great,' he shouted. 'It's warm. The sun's warmed the water up. Come on.'

Holly hesitated. Under her jeans she'd got leggings on. They were tight; they'd be OK to swim in. On top, under her sweater, she'd got a baggy T-shirt. That'd be OK too. So she swam out after him. The coldness of the water shocked her rigid at first, but he was right, it was quite warm when you got used to it, and the waterfall felt tepid, like a warm shower.

They sat there for ages, not talking, just enjoying the lovely feel of the rushing water on them as they swished their toes in the dark pool. Then Jake pressed her arm and whispered, 'Look, don't move,' as a great grey bird landed with silent grace on a rock that jutted out below them where the water shallowed out, showing up the pebbles on the bed of the stream.

The heron didn't do anything. It didn't peck around, or fish or call frantically to its mate, it just *was*, in the most perfect stillness, and, watching it, Holly felt she would always remember this moment, sitting there with Jake as the water poured over them, their toes in the water, sunlight dappling the pool, this marvellous large bird.

After they'd watched it for a bit it flew away. Jake slid back into the water. 'I'm getting out,' he said. 'I'm going to dry myself up in that field. So if you want to have a wash, I mean *properly*, I won't look.'

Holly was touched by his grunting embarrassment. When he'd gone she swam back to where she'd left her clothes, stripped off the wet ones and got into the water again, soaping herself all over, rinsing off, then rubbing herself dry with a rough blue towel she'd nicked from Muv's jumble box.

She was very cold as she pushed through the trees to find Jake, but she was exhilarated too, and he seemed in a better mood. Perhaps it was because he'd shared something secret and special with her. This was the place he used to come with his dad; he'd learned to swim in that pool.

'The heron was great, wasn't it?' he said as they made their way to the barn. 'There are loads of birds round here; Dad used to watch them for hours.' He shivered suddenly. 'I could do with a hot drink. Perhaps we could buy some cocoa. We need to go shopping. We've hardly got any food left.'

She was going to ask him how that could be managed. They couldn't both go into town, not after what the pig boy had said. And how could she go anywhere, with no shoes? He went into the barn to get his rucksack and sort out his things, while she sat sunning herself on the grass and wondering what on earth they were going to do next. When he came out though, his face was tight and set; his good mood had absolutely evaporated.

'What's up?'

Jake dumped his rucksack in her lap. 'Look

through the side pockets, will you? Am I going mad or something?'

Holly looked, carefully. Both pockets were empty apart from a torn, sticky polythene bag, two spent matches and some fluff.

'There's nothing here.'

'Exactly.'

'What am I supposed to be looking for?'

'The money. It was in that bag.'

'*All* of it?'

'Yeah.' Jake stared at his boots.

Holly's mouth fell open. 'But we − you said − *why didn't you put it somewhere else, you fool?* That boy *saw* you get it out of the rucksack. He was *watching* you.' She was really shouting at him. Her face was red, her tight curls shaking, her hands screwed up into hard little bunches in desperation.

'Forgot, didn't I?' he mumbled. 'I meant to do it, but then I forgot. To tell the truth, I really didn't think he'd come back. Sorry.'

'Sorry? SORRY?' she yelled. 'What good is that now, being sorry? You amaze me,' she went on. 'You just amaze me. How could you be so stupid, so . . . so pigheaded? No. I take that back. Those pigs down there have got more sense.'

There was a pause, then Jake said, 'Sorry you think I'm a pig.' And he brushed his hand across his eyes. 'I wish you'd stop screaming at me.'

Holly made a huge effort to control herself and clamped her hands to her sides. He was twisting things again, to get sympathy. She'd never said he was a pig.

She *was* screaming at him though. It must remind him of his mother. 'Sorry,' she said, taking a step towards him. 'It's just . . . well, what are we going to *do*, for Heaven's sake? We can't live on thin air.'

S e v e n t e e n

Jake said, 'Well, for starters, we really do need some food. Did you bring any money, by any chance?'

Holly said, 'I've told you, my parents don't give me money.' She wanted to add, 'And I don't steal it, like you,' but she pressed her lips together, to stop the words coming out. He was still shaking slightly, after her outburst. She'd obviously said enough. 'We'll just have to go home,' she said.

'NO!' His voice was a shout. 'I'm *not* going home. We've only just come. We've not done anything yet. It could be great, here. Anyhow, I'm not going back to *her*.' His voice wobbled; Holly thought he was going to cry.

She wanted to make up, now, for losing her temper. She said steadily, 'I think your mother cares about you, Jake. I think she loves you, actually. She's got all those photographs of you, for a start.'

'Huh,' Jake sneered. 'Anyone can put photos up. What about loving me? I just don't *feel* she loves me. She's always going off.'

'Perhaps you drive her away. Perhaps you don't bother to talk to her. Do you? Talk to her I mean?'

'No, not much. She's on another planet from me.'

'Well, parents are. They can't help it. They've got so many worries, Jake. They've got to keep things going, whereas . . . well, look at us, we could do anything really, anything we liked. We're *free.*'

'No we're not. You can't do anything without money and we're flat broke at this moment,' he said gloomily.

'Is that why you stole the church plate then, to get money to be free?'

He was silent and pulled lumps of turf up, shredding them in his hands. 'S'pose so.' She looked at him. She was quite certain, now, that he'd not broken into Farve's safe. It was all talk.

She said, 'You didn't steal it, did you? That money you brought all came from the cash machine didn't it? You got it out with your mother's card.'

He turned bright red. 'Well, what if I did? She owes me something. She owes me a lot. And she left the letter with the code on lying round when her new card came. Silly cow.'

'Who *did* get into my father's safe then?'

'How should I know? Someone gave it to him didn't they? Someone must have known the number, to get the door open. It wasn't me.'

'I know it wasn't. I've known all along.' She felt very sorry for him. He'd wanted her to think he'd pulled off a really brilliant grown-up trick, when all the time it was sordid and petty, reading his mother's mail and just going to a cashpoint and stealing her money. But *why* did he steal things and why did he want to *have* things? There was a kind of emptiness in Jake, something that nothing he did could satisfy, a kind of terrible longing.

It was starting to rain. He got up and began to make his way down the field towards the stream. 'I'm going to see if I can get your shoes. Don't you come. There might be people around.' And he disappeared over the stone wall.

While he was away she had a thorough tidy-up in the barn. When she'd rearranged the few things they'd brought she decided to go through her clothes. Folded up inside the pocket of the windcheater she'd borrowed from Rachel was a very thin, bright-red cagoule, with a hood. That was good, because the windcheater itself was thick and would take hours to dry if she got rained on. This could go on top of it.

She shook it out and pulled it over her head.

There were pockets on each side and a zipped pocket along the front. She unzipped it and felt inside, bringing out a small ball of paper. Sweet wrappers no doubt. Rachel was a bit of a pig with sweets. But it wasn't a sweet wrapper, it was a ten-pound note, all screwed up.

She smoothed it out on her knee and inspected it carefully, just to make sure it was real and not something out of a children's game. 'Look what I've found,' she yelled, waving it as Jake came back up the field. 'It was inside this cagoule. I found one stuffed inside the pocket of Rachel's windcheater.' Muv, no doubt, would have called it 'a gift from God'. Holly wouldn't go that far, but she did feel it was somehow remarkable to have found the money. At least it meant they could get a square meal inside them before they went home. For home was where she was heading, in her mind. Jake didn't know what he was doing, she'd decided. She was going to organize him from now on.

He didn't seem all that interested in the money. He was wet through. He'd fallen in the stream. 'Your shoes floated away,' he said. 'I climbed out on to a branch, but when I dislodged them the water got them. They've gone. There was nothing I could do. Anyhow, I nicked these.' He held out a pair of black gym shoes.

'But I can't —'

'Listen, you can. You've got to have something to put on your feet. They're ancient. They're for paddling in, I should think. They were on the grass outside one of the tents. We'll put them back when we've bought you something else.'

Silently she squeezed into the shabby black pumps. They were at least two sizes too small but they *were* shoes, and better than going round with what now looked like rags wrapped round her feet.

'Thanks,' she said flatly. 'What next? It's raining.'

'Put that cagoule back on and we'll make a start.'

'Where are we going?'

'To get you some proper shoes and to find us something decent to eat. I'm nearly out of fags as well.'

'All on ten pounds?'

Jake said nothing, but he was wearing his old, determined look again. Holly hadn't seen that for some time. She set off behind him, keeping to the stone wall that bordered the field. If he started stealing things when they reached the town, or wherever they were going, she'd just abandon him. She could always try hitching a lift back to Darnley.

It was a very long walk, not the way they had come on the first day, to the place where they'd got off the train, but over bigger hills in quite the opposite direction, and not in sun this time, but in driving rain.

For once she didn't mind that Jake was a slow walker, because the little black gym shoes were crippling her feet and she could only hobble. Every time they heard a car engine he made her duck down behind the stone wall that ribboned over the fell-side, on and on and out of sight. He was frightened that the thief, the pig boy, had been gossiping and that people were after them. When the road was empty they still walked separately, Jake always a little bit ahead of her, smoking half a cigarette, then chucking it away.

She hobbled along in silence, locked in her own world, thinking more and more of the people she'd left at home, feeling guilty and sad, wanting to see Muv and Farve again in spite of what they'd done. This was no kind of freedom, dodging the cars, hiding behind walls, sitting holed up for hours in a chilly barn in the middle of nowhere. It felt like escaping from a prison, like being on the run. And it didn't seem to cheer Jake up, this running away. Most of the time they'd been together he'd been pretty miserable.

The town they were heading for was in another valley, and when they'd struggled to the top of the pass they ought to be able to see it, Jake told her. It had a fabulous fish and chip shop, he said; they could go in there, so long as they sat separately from one another. Her mouth started to water at the very mention of chips, after the tuna and lukewarm beans.

'Oh,' Jake said, then, 'Oh, *hell.*' He'd scrambled up a bank to get a better view of the town. It was there all right, but between them and it was a great sheet of water. The road just vanished into it, then reappeared on the far side, near a church with a squat, stubby tower. 'I'd forgotten. Those fields always get flooded when it rains, and it rained a lot last night.'

'What are we going to do then, swim?' The pain in Holly's feet was really agonizing now and hunger was ripping through her. She could almost smell hot chips, vinegar and tomato ketchup floating up to her on the wind.

'Funny, aren't you?' Jake's voice was tight with anger. 'We can walk it, but we'll have to go the long way round. It's just a bit slower, that's all.'

They set off again. Even the clear road was flooded. The water lapped Jake's boots and completely covered the tight black gym shoes. But by now Holly had almost ceased to feel that she had any feet. Other walkers, expertly equipped with boots and maps and neat little rucksacks, strode smartly past giving her funny looks. But she was past caring. She limped on, sustained by a vision of steaming food heaped up on a plate, though the road was so long she was beginning to think it was a mirage and that there was no town, no café, no chips, only this endless tramp over hard roads in the face of a biting wind.

At last though, they squelched down the high street of a little town. Ordinariness, the usual shop-fronts, most exhibiting 'closed' notices. One sold papers and sweets, plastic footballs swinging in a net inside the doorpost. Another sold buckets, brooms and bumper cartons of soap powder. There was a bank and a butcher's, and a little supermarket called 'Eileen's', which was open. Then, at the top of the street, next to the stubby church, oh, bliss, a peeling sign swung in the wind. 'Fat Jack's', it said, 'Fish 'n Chips'. This place was open too.

She said faintly, 'I've got to sit down, my feet really hurt me. I think I've lost my circulation.'

'Not yet,' Jake said, and his voice was nasty, more like a snarl. All of a sudden he seemed desperate. 'We've got to shop first. It's nearly closing-time.'

'No. I'm sitting down.'

Jake stared at her, pinched his lips together and took a deep breath. 'OK. Give me that tenner then.'

'I can't. What if they make me pay for the chips before you get back?'

He hesitated, then dug into a pocket. 'Here, I

found this.' And he pressed three coins into her hand. 'I'm going to the shops, before they close. That'll buy you fish and chips. I'll see you.' Reluctantly she handed over her money, and he disappeared.

Slowly, Holly turned her limping steps towards Fat Jack's, looking at the two pound-coins and the fifty-pence piece that were sticking to her wet palm. He was a cheat. He'd not said he had this money. He must have been planning to keep quiet about it, to get something for himself, cigarettes, presumably. In that moment she felt that she hated him. They'd run away, hadn't they? They were supposed to share things. She felt she'd never trust him again, not after this. And what had he been so anxious to buy at the shops? Full of doubt and disappointment, she pushed the door of the café open and stumbled into a warm, greasy fug.

She was in luck. The place was full and it smelt of wet socks and rubber. Almost everybody seemed to be a hiker and there were anoraks and rucksacks all over the place. A radio was standing on the counter, with faint pop music drifting out of it, and behind the counter stood a tall, thin man with sleeked-back grey hair. If this was Fat Jack, he'd been on a mega-diet.

She could only see one free seat, right at the back next to a fruit machine, so she dumped her anorak on it, pushed her way to the front and asked for fish and chips. She spoke in a mumble and kept her face turned away from Fat Jack. Their photo might have been in the paper, or on TV. But the man was very busy examining his latest batch of chips and shouting instructions to a shrivelled little woman in a red turban who was loading plates with food. He didn't seem interested in Holly. He just took her money and gave her a slip of paper with a number on. 'I'll call you when your order's ready,' he said rather grandly. She'd only asked for a small helping, in case Jake spent the whole of the ten-pound note.

When he came in he was carrying a bulging plastic carrier-bag. He looked carefully round the crowded café, then squeezed up beside her and took a handful of chips. 'Hey,' she said, 'get your own.' The fish and chips tasted glorious. She wanted them to last for ever. She felt she couldn't spare a crumb of them.

'Can't.'

'What about the ten pounds?'

'Spent it.'

'What on?'

He hesitated. 'Things . . . things we needed.'

'Did you get a torch?' One of the things she didn't like about the barn was having to do everything in the dark. She'd twice grazed her legs on the stone steps and she got nervous of all the rustling noises. If there were rats and mice, and there had to be, in a place like that, she'd prefer to see them for herself. At least she could aim a shoe at them. No, not a shoe. She didn't have any shoes. These horrible black pumps were going back to the camp-site; someone might love them. Anyhow, she didn't want to wear stolen shoes.

'No,' he said. 'Torches are too expensive. I got candles.'

'Is that safe?'

'Course,' he said scornfully. 'Listen, have you got any money over?'

'A bit.' And she put it into his hand. He looked at the blackboard, then at the coins. 'Great. I can get some chips with this.' He was happy again. He'd bought his cigarettes, no doubt, and his candles to add to the romantic atmosphere in the draughty barn. Now he was in for a bag of Fat Jack's chips.

But he came back in a hurry, without them. 'C'mon,' he whispered, pulling at her. Bewildered, she followed him to the door. 'What's the hurry? You've not got your chips.'

'That radio was tuned into the local station,' he whispered to her, as more campers piled into the café, 'and someone was talking about *us*.'

Eighteen

It was getting dark as they squelched back through the flooded lanes and wearily started to climb the great fell that lay between them and their own valley, where the barn was. The cars that chugged past, their engines labouring as the slope got steeper, had got headlights on. It wasn't very late, but it was stormy, and the countryside, so beautiful until now, felt threatening to Holly, the rain-filled wind like an enemy.

She offered to carry the shopping bag, but Jake wouldn't let her. He was definitely unwilling to be parted from it. 'You didn't buy me any shoes, I suppose?' she said.

'How could I, with ten pounds? The only way I could get you shoes was to nick them. I thought about it. It would have been dead easy. The shops were full of trippers.' His eyes shone. He found stealing things thrilling. It gave him a kind of buzz.

'So why didn't you?'

'Well, you don't like me doing it, do you? You're such a goody-goody, you are. Actually, you make me sick, the way you go on. I went all the way to the camp-site for you, to get your bloody shoes — and it was your own stupid fault they'd got washed away — and when I couldn't reach them and brought you the others you just pulled a face. You weren't a bit grateful. You make me sick,' he repeated.

He lit a cigarette and started sucking on it furiously. His whole body was rigid with rage. He'd obviously been brooding about the things that irritated him for a long, long time. Now they were coming out, as if he was squeezing one of his great big angry spots. Well, she was angry too.

She said, in a quiet, reasonable voice that she knew would drive him mad, 'You make *me* sick. You behave like a pig. And your cigarettes make me sick, literally. I just don't know how you can do it, up in that barn. You make it stink. You stink yourself too. You don't seem to know about washing. And why do you have to live in such a hideous mess all the time? It's as if, as if you do it on principle. I think you're off your rocker. I'm not surprised your mother doesn't want to talk to you. I'm not surprised she'd rather have her boyfriends.'

There was silence. Then, the next minute, a chopping blow from the back of Jake's hand sent her tottering across the road. She staggered about, seeing stars, and a car coming down the hill sounded its horn furiously and swerved to avoid her. Then Jake was standing over her. He didn't try to help her to her feet and he didn't say he was sorry. He just said, 'Leave my mother out of it. She's had a horrible life. My father treats her like dirt. Say one more thing about my mother and I'll kill you!' Suddenly he started to cry, silently, by the side of the road, and Holly was crying too, not because he'd hit her, but because everything suddenly felt absolutely hopeless. It was dark and they had to go back to the menacing barn with its rustlings, to their damp sleeping-bags and to endless hours lying awake because they were too cold and hungry for good sleep to come to them. She wished with all her heart that she was back home, with Muv and Farve and N.O.P., with gentle, soft-faced Fat Nan and Doris. Yes, she even missed Doris.

She wiped her face with the back of her hand and sniffed hard. 'Come on,' she said to Jake, who was still crying. 'We've got to get back before it's completely dark. We'll never find our way otherwise.' She picked up the plastic shopping bag and this time he didn't try to stop her. He walked on ahead in total silence, rubbing at his face from time to time, then sobbing again. She'd never seen anyone cry like that before. It was as if he'd been waiting all his life to cry properly. And at this moment she couldn't go and comfort him. She was too full of her own worries and guilt to do that. Why on earth had they ever come?

In the bag was a white sliced loaf, spongy and cold, and a lump of orange cheese, some packets of cigarettes and a bottle of wine. Holly set everything out in a corner, by a candle they'd lit and stuck in a crack in the floor. She didn't say anything for a minute. She just looked at him, and at the bottle. 'Why on earth did you spend the money on wine?'

'Because I can't sleep,' he said. 'It's awful, lying awake all the time. Wine makes you sleepy.'

She didn't say anything, but she didn't understand. In the night his snoring had woken her up more than once. How could he say he'd never got any sleep? She drank a bit of the wine, but she didn't like it very much. It had a raw, sour taste. Jake seemed to enjoy it and drank a lot with his bread and cheese. He didn't smoke a cigarette though, and he treated her very respectfully, even carrying a candle down the steps for her when she wanted to go to the loo. She knew it was because of their quarrel on the road, when he'd hit her.

They got into their sleeping-bags and lay side by side in the darkness, watching the candlelight making its strange finger patterns on the knobbled wall. Before, they'd slept at opposite ends of the barn, but he'd pulled his things beside her now. He seemed to want to be close.

As they lay there they talked quietly, he about his parents and she about hers. He told her that his mother had trouble with her nerves and that this was the reason she was so crazy about the state of the house, and why she screamed at him when things got messed up. Sometimes, he said, she took pills to calm her down. It had been all right till his father left. He was weak, his father was. There was no denying it.

She told him about the vicarage and how she'd felt pushed out by all the drop-ins, how her parents were so busy helping people and doing good things they sometimes seemed to forget about her. She told him Muv was weak and didn't stick up for herself, but most of all she talked about Farve. She'd realized, since running away, just how much she wanted him to love her, but it felt as if there was a tight knot inside him, a knot of love that somehow couldn't be untied. It made him cold with people, cold and jerky, yet she knew he cared really, that he'd kill anyone who tried to harm someone in his family.

She knew now, beyond any doubt, that Muv and Farve were good people and she knew that she wanted to be with them, not stuck in this barn having an 'adventure'. She had decided that the reason family things fell apart, landing her with all the jobs and no attention from her parents, was that neither of them knew how to say 'no' to people, to the helpless, pathetic people who always seemed to end up at the vicarage. It wasn't right that she should feel so pushed out, but it didn't happen because they were bad, it happened because they were *good*.

It was all to do with this mysterious 'thing' that had happened to Farve when she was little when, one day, he went to a meeting and suddenly found he believed in God, and in Jesus Christ,and threw up his job so he could study, and work for the church. Dimly, she remembered a small, neat house in another town, a nice car, Farve in a smart suit, and Muv not so tired and worried-looking all the time. Dimmer than that was some idea she'd got from Muv that Farve had once been quite wild, and a trouble to his parents, like Auntie Linda, who'd run away. So her being friends with Jake must be a bit complicated for him. It was all right looking after dropouts, that was 'official', but when someone like a dropout got too friendly with his Holly . . . that was obviously scary for him.

'I think I understand my father now,' she said, 'now I've come away. I've been able to see him

properly. He *does* love me, only . . . Jake? JAKE!'
This was important, sharing Farve's life with someone. But Jake was snoring gently. He had fallen
asleep holding her hand. She too was drifting
towards unconsciousness and feeling more relaxed
than before, because at last she'd sorted it out
about Farve. And perhaps, too, it was because they
were leaving this place tomorrow. They'd agreed
they couldn't stay. She'd not said it was to go
home, but home was what she wanted now.

When she woke up there was an oblong of light
on the floor from the tiny window, cold, grey
light. So it was still early. But something was
wrong; she wasn't breathing properly, and the light
in the barn itself was wobbly. There was a haze in
the room, and a funny smell.

Jake's hand was still loosely in hers. They must
have been lying like that all night. Now she
snatched her fingers away, sat up and stared round
her. What she could smell was smoke. Something
in the room was on fire.

She struggled to her feet, kicking away the
sleeping-bag into a corner. There was smoke everywhere, coming up from the floor, and here and
there there were thin lines of flame, licking along
the edges of the old joists, starting to get a hold
on the corners of the room. The candle! It must

have been the fat yellow candle that they'd stuck in a crack between the floorboards. The last thing she'd seen as she'd drifted into sleep had been its flickering flame on the walls. She'd thought, 'Better put that out . . .' But sleep had overcome her.

Coughing and spluttering as the thick smoke swirled round her, she found her way to the tiny window, tore off the polythene bag they'd stuck over it and looked out. It was a still, damp morning and there were the pigs below, grubbing about unconcernedly. It was only a short distance from the window to the ground, and to safety, but there was no way either of them could get through that window. Jake was really skinny, he probably only weighed about eight stone, but that window wasn't meant for people to climb through. It was for hay, presumably, poked through with a pitchfork.

She went back to him, took him by the shoulders and shook him hard. 'Jake, JAKE! Wake up, we've got to get out of here. The candle's set the place on fire, all the straw's alight, and the floor. Wake UP!' But she couldn't wake him. He didn't even moan. If he'd not been warm, with his chest going in and out, she could have thought he was dead. It was all that wine he'd drunk, nearly a whole bottle. The aim of it, so he'd said, was to give him a good night's sleep. Well, it had done that, and worse. It seemed to have knocked him out cold.

174

She went back to the window. The smoke was getting worse. Then she tried to reach the door, but as she approached it there was a whooshing noise and a sheet of flame engulfed it. Terrified, she took hold of Jake, still inside his sleeping-bag, and dragged him across to the window. This part of the barn was the only place where stuff was not on fire. But the smoke and flames were spreading. It was only a matter of time before it reached them.

'Highly inflammable,' said the embroidered label on the sleeping-bag she'd borrowed from Rachel. She'd noticed that, when she'd rolled it into her rucksack. So it was no use beating out the flames with that. It could only make matters much worse. She looked wildly round her, feeling a rush of cold air, welcome in what was fast becoming a stifling heat. Over her head there was a hole. The roof of the barn was great slabs of stone, weighted down outside with smaller ones, to stop them moving when the snow came. One of the slabs was missing altogether, and another was cracked. It was a slightly bigger space than the window and it was their only chance.

In one corner was an ancient bedside table with a cracked top, covered with bird droppings. Heaven knew what it was doing in a barn. Jake had wanted to use it for a 'table', but she'd said no, it was too filthy, and he'd said she was just like his mother.

175

Now she dragged it through the smoke until it stood under the hole in the roof, climbed on to it, reached up until she could grab the rafters and gave an almighty pull. Seconds later she'd squeezed through and was sitting on the roof, pulling and heaving at the slab nearest to the hole, clawing at it with bleeding finger ends till she'd shifted it a little and made the hole bigger. Down below there was what sounded like a muffled explosion. She dropped down into the smoke again and saw her sleeping bag in flames. Jake was on his feet now, with the caterpillar folds of his bedding clinging to his ankles. He was staggering about, barely half awake. 'Holly,' he cried feebly, 'Holly, where are you? What's happening?' His voice sounded like that of a little helpless child.

'Over here, come *on*.' She grabbed him, jumped on to the table and heaved herself out again. Then she reached down inside, grasped his bony wrists and pulled for dear life. Bit by bit, and with agonizing slowness it seemed to her, Jake's head appeared above the smouldering rafters, then his arms, then the rest of him, his thin legs kicking the air as he came. One minute she was thinking of a man on the gallows, his legs kicking until all life had gone, the next she was thinking of the sick man whose friends had brought him to Jesus by making a hole in the roof. This was that story in reverse. It was the same though. It was the hole that had saved them, except that, as she slid down the roof with Jake and jumped the few remaining feet on to the ground, there was no kindly Lord to comfort and heal them. They were still on their own.

Her instinct was to get as far away from the burning barn as possible. She should tell someone, surely. She should go to the camp-site or to the pig boy's house. Jake seemed to be crying again. She supposed it was shock. She didn't feel anything. She couldn't, not yet. She put her arm round him and steered him away from the barn, out over the grass towards the pigs. As they walked there was an explosion behind them. She looked back. The roof of the barn was in flames, savage red against a marvellous pink and pearl sky.

She could not separate the low roar of the fire from the sound of the stream at the bottom of the field. Its soft burbling had comforted her as she'd lain awake at night, longing for home. But now another sound came in, voices, raised voices, shouts and exclamations floating across to them, and she saw the pig boy and a man with him, a man very like him, but fatter, with the same broad upturned nose and black holes for nostrils. Behind them came two policemen, and there were two other people. But she couldn't see them properly yet.

177

When the pig boy and his father saw the burning barn they started to run, lumbering right up to Jake and Holly, but ignoring them, pushing past, picking up planks and making for the barn, beating at the flames, shouting to one another, cursing. The policemen ran after them and together they attacked the fire. They took no notice at all of the two people they had brought with them, or of what was going on in the field with the pigs, who, perhaps because it was early and they weren't ready to eat yet, had gathered round curiously.

Mrs Tolland looked saggy and old. She was wearing a luminous green anorak and, for once, no make up. Her face was grey with tiredness. At first, when she saw Jake, she took a few steps towards him, raised both fists, as if she was going to hail blows upon him, then thrashed helplessly at the air. 'How *could* you,' she said in a shrill, high-pitched voice, 'how could you *do* this to me, Jake? I've been worried out of my mind.' Jake said nothing, took a step towards her and put his face against her green anorak, closing his eyes. For a second or two she did nothing. Then, slowly, she bowed her head over him and pulled him towards her. She seemed to understand, at last, that this wasn't a time for screaming.

Holly did not look at Farve at first, she looked at her feet. They were swollen, dirty and bare.

They were the feet of someone who'd run away and eaten pig food. She whispered, 'Is everyone all right at home?'

'Everyone's fine. James came back early, and we found somewhere else for the Sinclairs. We want to redecorate your room. I'd not realized how shabby it was, until your mother told me.'

She looked into his face. He too looked tired and grey and he'd not shaved. He'd got a bit of a beard. She liked it, it made him look like a Bible person. She said, 'Jake didn't take that gold plate.'

'I know. The police tracked it down. It's in the bank again. Don't worry about it now.'

Silence fell between them, the deep silence of the hills, which, for all the discomforts of the adventure, she had come to love. She said, 'It's really great here.'

Farve stared across at Jake and his mother. One of the policemen was now hovering behind them and Holly noticed that Mrs Tolland was clinging to her son, as if she feared they might snatch him away.

'Will he be all right?' her father said.

Holly shrugged. Typical Farve, focusing on someone else, wriggling away from the real problem, the problem of her and him.

She said, 'I don't know. I feel sorry for him. He's not got much to look forward to, has he?'

'No. That's what your mother said. I've not been too friendly to him, have I? Does he get on with James? D'you think he'd like to do more things with us? I thought we might have a bit of a holiday up here, stay in a cottage or something. He could come with us.'

'What about the drop-ins?' Holly said suspiciously. All this sounded a bit too good to be true.

'The house is empty. We're having a break from them. It's just *us*, for now. And Jake's welcome. It'd be good having him around more, with James away at school. Your mother − she's a wonderful woman − it was only when your mother said . . . and when we couldn't find you . . . Oh, God.' And he brushed a hand across his face, and sat down.

Holly moved a few inches closer to him, to where he sat hunched up on the grass. But she still felt very separate. As yet she could not bring herself to sit down beside him.

So Muv, at last, had said her piece. Muv the doormat, who had always stuck up for him, had obviously stuck up for Holly and Jake. She should have said, 'Three Cheers!' but she felt so sorry for Farve.

He said, 'Jake's a clever boy. We found your newspaper, the *Daily Scream*. We went snooping, in your bedrooms, to try and work out where you'd gone. "Are your parents snoopers?"' And the ghost of a smile passed over his face. 'It's a brilliant idea. I think you ought to publish it. Jake's mother knows someone who could print it for you. You could sell it at school.'

She was amazed. 'Do you really think it's brilliant? I thought you might be angry.'

'No, love. I'm not angry. I'm just . . .' But for the second time he couldn't speak.

The two policemen, followed by the pig boy and his father, were going off down the hill. The barn was safe, it seemed, in spite of a lot of smoke. One of them exchanged glances with Farve. 'Give us a minute,' Farve said. 'We'll be down.'

'OK, Rev. Glad you found the little horrors.'

'What'll happen to us?' Holly said.

'Nothing. We'll have to pay for the barn roof, that's all.'

'But what about running away?'

'They're not interested, love. It's all *right*. In the great scheme of things two children doing a bunk for a few days is, well . . .' And he smiled. 'It's kids' stuff to the police. For me though . . .' And he made room for her beside him on the grass. 'For me and your mother . . . Come here, Holly, come here to me.'

At first they both felt rigid with each other, then something in the air softened, and they came close. She said, 'I'm sorry, Farve.'

181

He said, 'I'm sorry too, really I am. And it *is* going to be different. I'm going to, well, this year I thought we'd have Christmas.'

'*Christmas?*' Holly muttered vaguely. What was that? There were other things to think about first. She didn't want to think about Christmas for at least a hundred years.

Suddenly a great weariness came over her and she sagged down against her father, on to her knees. She couldn't stand up any more. And his arms crept round her, nervously at first, but at last becoming firm and strong. The father was comforting his child.